HAWKMOON

THE
JEWEL IN THE SKULL

BY THE SAME AUTHOR

THE ETERNAL CHAMPIONS

The Eternal Champion
Von Bek
Hawkmoon
A Nomad of the Time Streams
Elric: The Song of the Black Sword
The Roads Between the Worlds
Corum: The Coming of Chaos
Sailing to Utopia

Kane of Old Mars
The Dancers at the End of Time
Elric: The Stealer of Souls
The Prince with the Silver Hand
Legends from the End of Time
Earl Aubec
Count Brass

OTHER NOVELS

Gloriana; or, The Unfulfill'd Queen
The Brothel in Rosenstrasse
Mother London
Blood
Fabulous Harbours
The War Amongst the Angels
Karl Glogauer novels
Behold the Man
Breakfast in the Ruins

Cornelius novels
The Cornelius Chronicles (Avon)
A Cornelius Calendar
Colonel Pyat novels
Byzantium Endures
The Laughter of Carthage
Jerusalem Commands
The Vengeance of Rome

SHORT STORIES AND GRAPHIC NOVELS

Casablanca
Lunching with the Antichrist (Mark Ziesing)
The Swords of Heaven, The Flowers of Hell (with
    Howard V. Chaykin)

The Crystal and the Amulet (with James
    Cawthorn)
Stormbringer (with P. Craig Russell), etc.

NONFICTION

The Retreat from Liberty
Letters from Hollywood (illus. M. Foreman)

Wizardry and Wild Romance
Death Is No Obstacle (with Colin Green
    etc.)

EDITOR

New Worlds
The Traps of Time
The Best of New Worlds
Best SF Stories from New Worlds
New Worlds: An Anthology

Before Armageddon
England Invaded
The Inner Landscape
The New Nature of the Catastrophe

RECORDS

With THE DEEP FIX:
The New Worlds Fair (Griffin Records)
Dodgem Dude
The Brothel in Rosenstrasse etc.

With HAWKWIND:
Warrior on the Edge of Time
Sonic Attack
Zones
Out and Intake
Live Chronicles (Griffin Records, USA) etc.

Also work with Blue Öyster Cult,
Robert Calvert, etc.

HAWKMOON

THE
JEWEL IN THE SKULL

MICHAEL MOORCOCK

A TOM DOHERTY ASSOCIATES BOOK

NEW YORK

HAWKMOON: THE JEWEL IN THE SKULL

Copyright © 1967, 1977 by Michael and Linda Moorcock

Illustrations © 2009 by Vance Kovacs

A Tor Book
Published by Tom Doherty Associates, LLC
175 Fifth Avenue
New York, NY 10010

www.tor-forge.com

Tor® is a registered trademark of Tom Doherty Associates, LLC.

ISBN 978-0-7653-2473-3

First Tor Trade Paperback Edition: January 2010

Printed in the United States of America

0 9 8 7 6 5 4 3 2 1

For Dave Brock

BOOK ONE

Then the Earth grew old, its landscapes mellowing and
showing signs of age, its ways becoming whimsical
and strange in the manner of a man in his last
years . . .

—*The High History of the Runestaff*

1

COUNT BRASS

Count Brass, Lord Guardian of Kamarg, rode out on a horned horse one morning to inspect his territories. He rode until he came to a little hill, on the top of which stood a ruin of immense age. It was the ruin of a Gothic church whose walls of thick stone were smooth with the passing of winds and rains. Ivy clad much of it, and the ivy was of the flowering sort so that at this season purple and amber blossoms filled the dark windows, in place of the stained glass that had once decorated them.

His rides always brought Count Brass to the ruin. He felt a kind of fellowship with it, for, like him, it was old; like him, it had survived much turmoil, and, like him, it seemed to have been strengthened rather than weakened by the ravages of time. The hill on which the ruin stood was a waving sea of tall, tough grass, moved by the wind. The hill was surrounded by the rich, seemingly infinite marshlands of Kamarg—a lonely landscape populated by wild white bulls, horned horses, and giant scarlet flamingoes so large they could easily lift a grown man.

The sky was a light grey, carrying rain, and from it shone sunlight of watery gold, touching the count's armour of burnished brass and making it flame. The count wore a huge broadsword at his hip, and a plain helmet, also of brass, was on his head. His whole body was sheathed in heavy brass, and even his gloves and boots were of brass links sewn upon leather. The count's body was broad, sturdy and tall, and he had a great, strong head whose tanned face might also have been moulded of brass. From this head stared two steady eyes of golden brown. His hair was red as his heavy moustache. In Kamarg and beyond, it was not unusual to hear the legend that the count was not a true man at all but a living statue in brass, a Titan, invincible, indestructible, immortal.

But those who knew Count Brass knew well enough that he was a man in every sense—a loyal friend, a terrible foe, given much to laughter yet capable of ferocious anger, a drinker of enormous capacity, a trencherman of not indiscriminate tastes, a swordsman and a horseman without peer, a sage in the ways of men and history, a lover at once tender and savage. Count Brass, with his rolling, warm voice and his rich vitality, could not help but be a legend, for if the man was exceptional, then so were his deeds.

Count Brass stroked the head of his horse, rubbing his gauntlet between the animal's sharp, spiral horns and looking to the south, where the sea and sky met far away. The horse grunted with pleasure, and Count Brass smiled, leaned back in his saddle, and flicked the reins to make the horse descend the hill and head along the secret marsh path toward the northern towers beyond the horizon.

The sky was darkening when he reached the first tower and saw its guardian, an armoured silhouette against the skyline, keeping his vigil. Though no attack had been made on Kamarg since Count Brass had come to replace the former, corrupt Lord Guardian, there was now some slight danger that roaming armies (those whom the Dark Empire of the west had defeated) might wander into the domain looking for towns and villages to loot. The guardian, like all his fellows, was equipped with a flamelance of baroque design, a sword four feet long, a tamed riding flamingo tethered to one side of the battlements, and a heliograph device to signal information to nearby towers. There were other weapons in the towers, weapons the count himself had had built and installed, but the guardians knew only their method of operation; they had never seen them in action. Count Brass had said that they were more powerful than any weapons possessed even by the Dark Empire of Granbretan, and his men believed him and were a little wary of the strange machines.

The guardian turned as Count Brass approached the tower. The man's face was almost hidden by his black iron helmet, which curved around his cheeks and over his nose. His body was swathed in a heavy leather cloak. He saluted, raising his arm high.

Count Brass raised his own arm. "Is all well, guardian?"

"All well, my lord." The guardian shifted his grip on his flamelance and turned up the cowl of his cloak as the first drops of rain began to fall. "Save for the weather."

Count Brass laughed. "Wait for the mistral and then complain." He guided his horse away from the tower, making for the next.

The mistral was the cold, fierce wind that whipped across Kamarg for months on end, its wild keening a continuous sound until spring. Count Brass loved to ride through it when it was at its height, the force of it lashing at his face and turning his bronze tan to a glowing red.

Now the rain splashed down on his armour, and he reached behind his saddle for his cloak, tugging it about his shoulders and raising the hood. Everywhere through the darkening day reeds bent in the breeze-borne rain, and there was a patter of water on water as the heavy drops splashed into the lagoons, sending out ceaseless ripples. Above, the clouds banked blacker, threatening to release a considerable weight, and Count Brass decided he would forego the rest of his inspection until the next day and instead return to his castle at Aigues-Mortes, a good four hours' ride through the twisting marsh paths.

He urged the horse back the way they had come, knowing that the beast would find the paths by instinct. As he rode, the rain fell faster, making his cloak sodden. The night closed in rapidly until all that could be seen was a solid wall of blackness broken only by the silver traceries of rain. The horse moved more slowly but did not pause. Count Brass could smell its wet hide and promised it special treatment by the grooms when they reached Aigues-Mortes. He brushed water from its mane with his gloved hand and tried to peer ahead, but could see only the reeds immediately around him, hear only the occasional maniacal cackle of a mallard, flapping across a lagoon pursued by a water-fox or an otter. Sometimes he thought he saw a dark shape overhead and felt the swish of a swooping flamingo making for its communal nest or recognized the squawk of a moorhen battling for its life with an owl. Once, he caught a flash of white in the darkness and listened to the blundering passage of a nearby herd of white bulls as they made for firmer land to sleep; and he noticed the sound, a little later, of a marsh-bear stalking the herd, his breath whiffling, his feet making only the slightest noise as he carefully padded across the quaking surface of the mud. All these sounds were familiar to Count Brass and did not alarm him.

Even when he heard the high-pitched whinny of frightened horses and heard their hoofbeats in the distance he was not unduly perturbed until his own horse stopped dead and moved uncertainly. The horses were coming directly toward him, charging down the narrow causeway in panic. Now Count Brass could see the leading stallion, its eyes rolling in fear, its nostrils flaring and snorting.

Count Brass yelled and waved his arms, hoping to divert the stallion, but it was too panic-stricken to heed him. There was nothing else to do. Count Brass yanked at the reins of his mount and sent it into the marsh, hoping desperately that the ground would be firm enough to hold them at least until the herd had passed. The horse stumbled into the reeds, its hoofs seeking purchase in the soft mud; then it had plunged into water and Count Brass saw spray fly and felt a wave hit his face, and the horse was swimming as best it could through the cold lagoon, bravely carrying its armoured burden.

The herd had soon thundered past. Count Brass puzzled over what had panicked them so, for the wild horned horses of Kamarg were not easily disturbed. Then, as he guided his horse back toward the path, there came a sound that immediately explained the commotion and sent his hand to the hilt of his sword.

It was a slithering sound, a slobbering sound; the sound of a baragoon—the marsh gibberer. Few of the monsters were left now. They had been the creations of the former Guardian, who had used them to terrorize the people of Kamarg before Count Brass came. Count Brass and his men had all but destroyed the race, but those which remained had learned to hunt by night and avoid large numbers of men at all costs.

The baragoon had once been men themselves, before they had been taken as slaves to the former Guardian's sorcerous laboratories and there transformed. Now they were monsters eight feet high and enormously broad, bile-coloured and slithering on their bellies through the marshlands; they rose only to leap upon and rend their prey with their steel-hard talons. When they did, on occasion, have the good fortune to find a man alone they would take slow vengeance, delighting in eating a man's limbs before his eyes.

As his horse regained the marsh path, Count Brass saw the baragoon ahead, smelled its stench, and coughed on the odour. His huge broadsword was now in his hand.

The baragoon had heard him and paused.

Count Brass dismounted and stood between his horse and the monster. He gripped his broadsword in both hands and walked, stiff-legged in his armour of brass, toward the baragoon.

Instantly it began to gibber in a shrill, repulsive voice, raising itself up and flailing with its talons in an effort to terrify the count. To Count Brass the apparition was not unduly horrific; he had seen much worse in his time. But he knew that his chances against the beast were slim, since the baragoon could see in the dark and the marsh was its natural environment. Count Brass would have to use cunning.

"You ill-smelling foulness!" (He spoke in an almost jocular tone.) "I am Count Brass, the enemy of your race. It was I who destroyed your evil kin and it is thanks to me that you have so few brothers and sisters these days. Do you miss them? Would you join them?"

The baragoon's gibbering shout of rage was loud but not without a hint of uncertainty. It shuffled its bulk but did not move toward the count.

Count Brass laughed. "Well, cowardly creation of sorcery—what's your answer?"

The monster opened its mouth and tried to frame a few words with its misshapen lips, but little emerged that could be recognized as human speech. Its eyes now did not meet Count Brass's.

Casually, Count Brass dug his great sword into the ground and rested his gauntleted hands upon the cross-piece. "I see you are ashamed of terrorizing the horses I protect, and I am in good humour, so I will pity you. Go now and I'll let you live a few more days. Stay, and you die this hour."

He spoke with such assurance that the beast dropped back to the ground, though it did not retreat. The count lifted up his sword and walked impatiently forward. He wrinkled his nose against the stench of the monster, paused, and waved the thing away from him. "Into the swamp, into the slime where you belong! I am in a merciful mood tonight."

The baragoon's wet mouth snarled, but still he hesitated.

Count Brass frowned a little, judging his moment, for he had known the baragoon would not retreat so easily. He lifted his sword. "Will this be your fate?"

The baragoon began to rise on its hind legs, but Count Brass's

timing was exactly right. He was already swinging the heavy blade into the monster's neck.

The thing struck out with both taloned hands, its gibbering cry a mixture of hatred and terror. There was a metallic squeal as the talons scored gashes in the count's armour, sending him staggering backward. The monster's mouth opened and closed an inch from the count's face, its huge black eyes seeming to consume him with their rage. He staggered back, taking his sword with him. It came free. He regained his footing and struck again.

Black blood pumped from the wound, drenching him. There was another terrible cry from the beast, and its hands went to its head, trying desperately to hold it in place. Then the baragoon's head flopped half off its shoulders, blood pumped again, and the body fell.

Count Brass stood stock still, panting heavily, staring with grim satisfaction at the corpse. He wiped the creature's blood fastidiously from him, smoothed his heavy moustache with the back of his hand, and congratulated himself that he appeared to have lost none of his guile or his skill. He had planned every moment of the encounter, intending from the first to kill the baragoon. He had kept the creature bewildered until he could strike. He saw no wrong in deceiving it. If he had given the monster a fair fight, it was likely that he, and not the baragoon, would now be lying headless in the mud.

Count Brass took a deep breath of the cold air and moved forward. With some effort he managed to dislodge the dead baragoon with his booted foot, sending it slithering into the marsh.

Then Count Brass remounted his horned horse and rode back to Aigues-Mortes without further incident.

2

YISSELDA AND BOWGENTLE

Count Brass had led armies in almost every famous battle of his day; he had been the power behind the thrones of half the rulers of Europe, a maker and a destroyer of kings and princes. He was a master of intrigue, a man whose advice was sought in any affair involving political struggle. He had been, in truth, a mercenary; but he had been a mercenary with an ideal, and the ideal had been to set the continent of Europe toward unification and peace. Thus he had, from preference, leagued himself with any force he judged capable of making some contribution to this cause. Many a time he had refused the offer to rule an empire, knowing that this was an age when a man could make an empire in five years and lose it in six months, for history was still in a state of flux and would not settle in the count's lifetime. He sought only to guide history a little in the course he thought best.

Tiring of wars, of intrigue, and even, to some extent, of ideals, the old hero had eventually accepted the offer of the people of Kamarg to become their Lord Guardian.

That ancient land of marshes and lagoons lay close to the coast of the Mediterranean. It had once been part of the nation called France, but France was now two dozen dukedoms with as many grandiose names. Kamarg, with its wide, faded skies of orange, yellow, red, and purple, its relics of the dim past, its barely changing customs and rituals, had appealed to the old count and he had set himself the task of making his adopted land secure.

In his travels in all the Courts of Europe, he had discovered many secrets, and thus the great, gloomy towers that ringed the borders of Kamarg now protected the territory with more potent, less-recognizable weaponry than broadswords or flame-lances.

On the southern borders, the marshes gradually gave way to sea, and sometimes ships stopped at the little ports, though travelers rarely disembarked. This was because of Kamarg's terrain. The wild landscapes were treacherous to those not familiar with them, and the marsh roads were hard to find; also, mountain ranges flanked its three sides on land. The man wishing to head inland disembarked farther east and took a boat up the Rhone. So Kamarg received little news from the outside world, and what it did receive was usually stale.

This was one of the reasons why Count Brass had settled there. He enjoyed the sense of isolation; he had been too long involved with worldly affairs for even the most sensational news to interest him much. In his youth he had commanded armies in the wars that constantly raged across Europe. Now, however, he was tired of all conflict and refused all requests for aid or advice that reached him, no matter what inducement was offered.

In the west lay the island empire of Granbretan, the only nation with any real political stability, with her half-insane science and her ambitions of conquest. Having built the tall, curved bridge of silver that spanned thirty miles of sea, the empire was bent on increasing her territories by means of her black wisdom and her war machines like the brazen ornithopters that had a range of more than a hundred miles. But even the encroachment of the Dark Empire into the mainland of Europe did not greatly disturb Count Brass; it was a law of history, he believed, that such things must happen, and he saw the ultimate benefits that could result from a force, no matter how cruel, capable of uniting all the warring states into one nation.

Count Brass's philosophy was the philosophy of experience, the philosophy of a man of the world rather than a scholar, and he saw no reason to doubt it, while Kamarg, his sole responsibility, was strong enough to resist even the full might of Granbretan.

Having nothing, himself, to fear from Granbretan, he watched with a certain remote admiration the cruel and efficient manner in which the nation spread her shadow farther and farther across Europe with every year that passed.

Across Scandia and all the nations of the North the shadow fell, along a line marked by famous cities: Parye, Munchein, Wien, Krahkov, Kerninsburg (itself a foothold in the mysterious land of Muskovia). A great semi-circle of power in the main continental landmass; a semicircle that grew wider almost every day and must soon touch the northernmost princedoms of Italia,

Magyaria, and Slavia. Soon, Count Brass guessed, the Dark Empire's power would stretch from the Norwegian Sea to the Mediterranean, and only Kamarg would not be under its sway. It was partly with this knowledge in mind that he had accepted the Lord Guardianship of the territory when its previous Guardian, a corrupt and spurious sorcerer from the land of the Bulgars, had been torn to pieces by the native guardians whom he had commanded.

Count Brass had made Kamarg secure from attack from outside and from menace from within. There were few baragoons left to terrorize the people of the many small villages, and other terrors had been dealt with also.

Now the count dwelt in his warm castle at Aigues-Mortes, enjoying the simple, rural pleasures of the land, while the people were, for the first time in many years, free from anxiety.

The castle, known as Castle Brass, had been built some centuries before on what had then been an artificial pyramid rising high above the centre of the town. But now the pyramid was hidden by earth in which had been planted grass and gardens for flowers, vines, and vegetables in a series of terraces. Here there were well-kept lawns on which the children of the castle could play or adults stroll, there were the grapevines that gave the best wine in Kamarg, and farther down grew rows of haricots and patches of potatoes, cauliflowers, carrots, lettuce, and many other common vegetables, as well as more exotic ones like the giant pumpkin-tomatoes, celery trees, and sweet ambrogines. There were also fruit trees and bushes that supplied the castle through most of the seasons.

The castle was built of the same white stone as the houses of the town. It had windows of thick glass (much of it painted fan-

cifully) and ornate towers and battlements of delicate workmanship. From its highest turrets it was possible to see most of the
territory it protected, and it was so designed that when the mistral
came an arrangement of vents, pulleys, and little doors could be
operated and the castle would sing so that its music, like that of
an organ, could be heard for miles on the wind.

The castle looked down on the red roofs of the town and at
the bullring beyond, which had originally been built, it was said,
many thousands of years ago by the Romanians.

Count Brass rode his weary horse up the winding road to the
castle and hallooed to the guards to open the gate. The rain was
easing off, but the night was cold and the count was eager to
reach his fireside. He rode through the great iron gates and into
the courtyard, where a groom took his horse. Then he plodded
up the steps, through the doors of the castle, down a short passage, and into the main hall.

There, a huge fire roared in the grate, and beside it, in deep,
padded armchairs, sat his daughter, Yisselda, and his old friend
Bowgentle. They rose as he entered, and Yisselda stood on tiptoe
to kiss his cheek, while Bowgentle stood by smiling.

"You look as if you could do with some hot food and a change
into something warmer than armour," said Bowgentle, tugging at
a bellrope. "I'll see to it."

Count Brass nodded gratefully and went to stand by the fire,
tugging off his helmet and placing it with a clank on the mantel.
Yisselda was already kneeling at his feet, tugging at the straps of his
greaves. She was a beautiful girl of nineteen, with soft rose-gold
skin and fair hair that was not quite blond and not quite auburn
but of a colour lovelier than both. She was dressed in a flowing

gown of flame-orange that made her resemble a fire sprite as she moved with graceful swiftness to carry the greaves to the servant who now stood by with a change of clothes for her father.

Another servant helped Count Brass shed his breastplate, back-plate, and other parts of his armour, and soon he was pulling on soft, loose trousers and shirt of white wool and wrapping a linen gown over that.

A small table, heavy with steaks of local beef, potatoes, salad, and a delicious thick sauce, was brought up to the fire, together with a flagon of mulled wine. Count Brass sat down with a sigh and began to eat.

Bowgentle stood by the fire watching him, while Yisselda curled up in the chair opposite and waited until he had taken the edge off his appetite.

"Well, my lord," said she with a smile, "how went the day? Is all our land secure?"

Count Brass nodded with mock gravity. "It would seem so, my lady, though I was not able to visit any of the northern towers but one. The rain came on, and I decided to return home." He told them about his encounter with the baragoon. Yisselda listened with wide eyes while Bowgentle looked somewhat grave, his kind, ascetic face bowed and his lips pursed. The famous philosopher-poet was not always approving of his friend's exploits and seemed to think that Count Brass brought such adventures upon himself.

"You'll recollect," said Bowgentle when the count had finished, "that I advised you this morning to travel with von Villach and some of the others." Von Villach was the count's chief lieutenant, a loyal old soldier who had been with him through most of his earlier exploits.

Count Brass laughed up at his dour-faced friend. "Von Villach? He's getting old and slow, and it would not be a kindness to take him out in this weather!"

Bowgentle smiled a little bleakly. "He's a year or two younger than yourself, Count . . ."

"Possibly, but could he defeat a baragoon single-handed?"

"That is not the point," Bowgentle continued firmly. "If you traveled with him and a party of men-at-arms you would not need to encounter a baragoon at all."

Count Brass waved a hand, dismissing the discussion. "I have to keep in practice; otherwise, I might become as moribund as von Villach."

"You have a responsibility to the people here, Father," Yisselda put in quietly. "If you were killed . . ."

"I shall not be killed!" The count smiled scornfully, as if death were something that only others suffered. In the firelight his head resembled the war mask of some ancient barbarian tribe, cast in metal, and it did seem in some way imperishable.

Yisselda shrugged. She had most of her father's qualities of character, including the conviction that there was little point indulging in arguments with such stubborn folk as Count Brass. Bowgentle had once written of her in a private poem, "She is like silk, both strong and soft," and looking at them now he noticed with quiet affection how the expression of one was reflected in the other.

Bowgentle changed the subject. "I heard today that Granbretan took the province of Köln not six months past," he said. "Their conquests spread like a plague."

"A healthy enough plague," Count Brass replied, settling back in his chair. "At least they establish order."

"Political order, perhaps," Bowgentle said with some fire, "but scarcely spiritual or moral. Their cruelty is without precedent. They are insane. Their souls are sick with a love for all that is evil and a hatred for all that is noble."

Count Brass stroked his moustache. "Such wickedness has existed before. Why, the Bulgar sorcerer who preceded me here was quite as evil as they."

"The Bulgar was an individual. So were the Marquis of Pesht, Roldar Nikolayeff, and their kind. But they were exceptions, and in almost every case the people they led revolted against them and destroyed them in time. But the Dark Empire is a *nation* of such individuals, and such actions as they commit are seen as natural. In Köln their sport was to crucify every girlchild in the city, make eunuchs of the boys, and have all adults who would save their lives perform lewd displays in the streets. That is no natural cruelty, Count, and was by no means their worst. Their entertainment is to debase all humanity."

"Such stories are exaggerated, my friend. You should realize that. Why, I myself have been accused of—"

"From all I hear," Bowgentle interrupted, "the rumours are not an exaggeration of the truth but a simplification. If their public activities are so terrible, what must their private delights be like?"

Yisselda shuddered. "I can't bear to think . . ."

"Exactly," Bowgentle said, turning to face her. "And few can bear to repeat what they have witnessed. The order they bring is superficial, the chaos they bring destroys men's souls."

Count Brass shrugged his broad shoulders. "Whatever they do, it is a temporary thing. The unification they force on the world is permanent, mark my words."

Bowgentle folded his arms across his black-clad chest. "The price is too heavy, Count Brass."

"No price is too heavy! What will you have? The princedoms of Europe dividing into smaller and smaller segments, war a constant factor in the life of the common man? Today few men can ever know peace of mind from cradle to grave. Things change and change again. At least Granbretan offers consistency!"

"And terror? I cannot agree with you, my friend."

Count Brass poured himself a goblet of wine, drank it down, and yawned a little. "You take these immediate events too seriously Bowgentle. If you had had my experience, you would realize that all such evil soon passes. A hundred years will see Granbretan a most upright and moral nation." Count Brass winked at his daughter, but she did not smile in return, seeming to agree with Bowgentle.

"Their sickness is too ingrained for a hundred years to cure it. That can be told from their appearance alone. Those jeweled beast-masks that they never doff, those grotesque clothes they wear in even the most extreme heat, their stance, their way of moving—all these things show them to be what they are. They are insane by heredity, and their progeny will inherit that insanity." Bowgentle struck his hand against a mantel pillar. "Our passivity is acquiescence in their deeds. We should—"

Count Brass rose from his chair. "We should go to our beds and sleep, my friend. Tomorrow we must appear at the bullring for the beginning of the festivities."

He nodded to Bowgentle, kissed his daughter lightly on the forehead, and left the hall.

3

BARON MELIADUS

At this season, the people of Kamarg began their great festival, the summer's work being over. Flowers covered the houses, the people wore clothes of richly embroidered silk and linen, young bulls charged through the streets at will, and the guardians paraded in all their martial finery. In the afternoons the bull contests took place in the ancient stone amphitheatre on the edge of the town.

The seats of the amphitheatre were of granite, arranged in tiers. Close to the steep wall of the ring itself, on the south side, was a covered area consisting of carved pillars and a red slate roof. This was hung with curtains of dark brown and scarlet. Within it sat Count Brass; his daughter, Yisselda; Bowgentle, and old von Villach.

From their box, Count Brass and his companions could see almost the whole of the amphitheatre as it began to fill, could hear the excited conversation and the thumps and snorts of the bulls behind the barricades.

Soon a fanfare sounded from the group of six guardians in plumed helmets and sky-blue cloaks on the far side of the amphitheatre. Their bronze trumpets echoed the noise of the bulls and the cheering crowd. Count Brass stepped forward.

The cheering grew louder as he appeared, smiling to the crowd and raising his hand in greeting. When the din had quieted, he began the traditional speech that would open the festival.

"Ancient people of Kamarg who were preserved by Fate from the blight of the Tragic Millennium; you who were given life, celebrate life today. You, whose ancestors were saved by the fierce mistral that cleansed the skies of the poisons that brought others death and malformation, give thanks in this festival for the coming of the Life Wind!"

Again the cheering broke out, and the fanfare blew for a second time. Then into the ring broke twelve huge bulls. They stampeded round and round the arena, tails high, horns gleaming, nostrils dilated, and red eyes shining. These were the prime fighting bulls of Kamarg, trained the year through for their performance today, when they would be matched against unarmed men who would try to snatch the several garlands that had been wound around their throats and horns.

Next, mounted guardians galloped out, waving to the crowd, and herded the bulls back into the enclosure under the amphitheatre.

When, with some difficulty, the guardians had got every bull into the enclosure, out rode the master of ceremonies, clad in a rainbow cloak, broad-brimmed hat of bright blue, and a golden megaphone through which he would announce the first contest.

Amplified by both the megaphone and the walls of the amphitheatre, the man's voice almost resembled the great roar of an angry bull. He announced first the name of the bull—Cornerouge of Aigues-Mortes, owned by Pons Yachar, the famous bull breeder—and then the name of the principal toreador, Mahtan Just of Arles. The master of ceremonies wheeled his horse about and disappeared. Almost at once, Cornerouge appeared from below the amphitheatre, his huge horns digging at the air, the scarlet ribbons that decorated them flying in the strong breeze.

Cornerouge was a huge bull, standing over five feet high. His tail lashed from side to side like a lion's; his red eyes glared at the shouting crowd that honoured him. Flowers were thrown into the ring and fell on his broad white back. He turned swiftly, pawing at the dust of the arena, trampling the flowers.

Then, lightly, unostentatiously, a slight, stocky figure appeared, dressed in a black cloak lined with scarlet silk, tight black doublet and trousers decorated with gold, knee-high boots of black leather, embellished with silver. His face was swarthy, young, alert. He doffed his wide-brimmed hat to the crowd, pirouetted, and faced Cornerouge. Though barely twenty, Mahtan Just had already distinguished himself in three previous festivals. Now the women threw flowers and he gallantly acknowledged them, blowing kisses even as he advanced toward the snorting bull and drew off his cloak in a graceful movement, displaying the red lining to Cornerouge, who took a few dancing steps forward, snorted again, and lowered his horns.

The bull charged.

Mahtan Just stepped aside and one hand reached out to pluck a ribbon from Cornerouge's horn. The crowd cheered and stamped. The bull turned speedily and charged again. Again Just stepped aside at the last possible moment, and again he plucked a ribbon. He held both trophies in his white teeth, and he grinned first at the bull, then at the crowd.

The first two ribbons, high on the bull's horns, were comparatively easy to win, and Just, knowing this, had won them almost casually. Now the lower ribbons must be taken from the horns, and this was much more dangerous.

Count Brass leaned forward in his box, staring admiringly at the toreador. Yisselda smiled. "Isn't he wonderful, Father? Like a dancer!"

"Aye, dancing with death," Bowgentle said with what amounted to self-mocking severity.

Old von Villach leaned back in his seat, appearing bored with the spectacle. It might simply have been that his eyes were not what they had once been and he did not want to admit it.

Now the bull was stampeding straight at Mahtan Just, who stood in its path with his hands on his hips, his cloak dropped in the dust. As the bull was almost upon him, Just leaped high into the air, his body grazing the horns, and somersaulted over Cornerouge, who dug his hoofs into the dust and snorted in puzzlement before turning his head at Just's laughing shout from behind him.

But before the bull could move his body, Just had jumped again, this time onto the back and, as the bull bucked madly beneath him, turned his attention to hanging on to one horn and disentangling a ribbon from the other. Just was soon dislodged, flung down to the ground, but he displayed another ribbon in his waving hand, rolled over, and just managed to get to his feet as the bull charged at him.

A tremendous noise broke out from the crowd as it clapped, shouted, and flung a veritable ocean of bright blooms into the ring. Just was now running lightly around the arena, pursued by the bull.

He paused, as if in deliberation, turned gradually on his heel, and seemed surprised to see the bull almost upon him.

Now Just jumped again, but a horn caught his coat and ripped it, sending him off-balance. One hand came down on the bull's back, and he vaulted to the ground but fell badly and rolled as the bull charged.

Just scrambled away, still in control of himself but unable to rise. The bull's head dipped, a horn lashed at the body. Droplets of blood sparkled in the sunlight, and the crowd moaned with a mixture of pity and bloodlust.

"Father!" Yisselda's hand gripped Count Brass's arm. "He'll be killed. Help him!"

Count Brass shook his head, although his body had moved involuntarily toward the ring. "It is his own affair. It is what he risks."

Just's body was now tossed high into the air, arms and legs loose like a rag doll's. Into the ring came the mounted guardians with long lances to goad the bull away from his victim.

But the bull refused to move, standing over Just's still body as a predatory cat might stand over the body of its prey.

Count Brass leaped over the side of the ring almost before he realized what he was doing. He ran forward in his armour of brass, ran at the bull like a metal giant.

The riders pulled their horses aside as Count Brass flung his body at the bull's head, grasping the horns in his great hands. Veins stood out on his ruddy face as he pushed the bull gradually back.

Then the head moved, and Count Brass's feet left the ground, but his hands kept their grip and he shifted his weight to one side, bearing the bull's head back so that gradually it seemed to bow.

There was silence everywhere. From the box, Yisselda, Bowgentle, and von Villach leaned forward, their faces pale. All in the amphitheatre were tense as Count Brass slowly exerted his strength.

Cornerouge's knees shook. He snorted and bellowed and his body bucked. But Count Brass, trembling with the effort of holding the horns, did not relent. His moustache and hair seemed to bristle, the muscles on his neck bulged and turned red, but gradually the bull weakened, and then slowly it fell to its knees.

Men ran forward to drag the wounded Just from the ring, but still the crowd was silent.

Then, with a great wrench, Count Brass flung Cornerouge over on his side.

The bull lay still, acknowledging its master; acknowledging that it was without question beaten.

Count Brass stepped back and the bull did not move, simply looked up at him through glazed, puzzled eyes, its tail shifting slightly in the dust, its huge chest rising and falling.

Now the cheering began.

Now the cheering rose in volume so that it seemed the whole world would hear it.

Now the crowd rose to its feet and hailed their Lord Guardian with unprecedented acclaim as Mahtan Just staggered forward clutching at his wound and gripped Count Brass's arm for a moment in gratitude.

And in the box Yisselda wept with pride and relief, and unabashed, Bowgentle wiped tears from his own eyes. Only von Villach did not weep, but his head nodded in grim approval of his master's feat.

Count Brass walked back toward the box, smiling up at his daughter and his friends. He gripped the wall and hauled himself back to his place. He laughed with rich enjoyment and waved at the crowd as they cheered him.

Then he raised his hand and addressed them as the cheering died.

"Do not give me the ovation—give it to Mahtan Just. He won the trophies. See"—he opened his palms and displayed them—"I have nothing!" There was laughter. "Let the festival continue." Count Brass sat down.

Bowgentle had recovered his composure. He leaned toward Count Brass. "So, my friend, do you still say you prefer to remain uninvolved in the struggles of others?"

Count Brass smiled at him. "You are indefatigable, Bowgentle. This, surely, was a local affair, was it not?"

"If your dreams of a united continent are still with you, then the affairs of Europe are *local* affairs." Bowgentle stroked his chin. "Are they not?"

Count Brass's expression became serious for an instant. "Perhaps . . ." he began, but then shook his head and laughed. "Oh, insidious Bowgentle, you still manage to confound me from time to time!"

But later, when they left the box and made their way back to the castle, Count Brass was frowning.

As Count Brass and his retinue rode into the castle courtyard, a man-at-arms ran forward, his pointing arm indicating an ornate carriage and a group of black, plumed stallions with saddles of unfamiliar workmanship, which the grooms were at that moment removing.

"Sire," the man-at-arms breathed, "there have come visitors to our castle while you were at the arena. Noble visitors, though I know not if you'll welcome them."

Count Brass looked hard at the carriage. It was of beaten metal, of dark gold, steel, and copper, inlaid with mother-of-pearl, silver, and onyx. It was fashioned to resemble the body of a grotesque beast, with its legs extending into claws, which clutched the wheel shafts. Its head was reptilian, with ruby eyes, hollowed out from above to form a seat for the coachman. On the doors was an elaborate coat of arms displaying many quarterings in which were strange-looking animals, weapons, and symbols of an obscure but disturbing nature. Count Brass recognized the design of the carriage and the coat of arms. The first was the workmanship of the mad smiths of Granbretan; the second was the coat of arms of one of that nation's most powerful and infamous nobles.

"It is Baron Meliadus of Kroiden," Count Brass said as he dismounted. "What business could bring such a great lord to our little province?" He spoke with some irony, but he seemed disturbed. He glanced at Bowgentle as the philosopher-poet came and stood beside him.

"We will treat him courteously, Bowgentle," said the count warningly. "We will show him all Castle Brass's hospitality. We have no quarrel with the Lords of Granbretan."

"Not at this moment, perhaps," said Bowgentle, speaking with evident restraint.

With Yisselda and von Villach behind them, Count Brass and Bowgentle ascended the steps and entered the hall, where they found Baron Meliadus waiting for them alone.

The baron was almost as tall as Count Brass. He was dressed all in gleaming black and dark blue. Even his jeweled animal mask, which covered the whole of his head like a helmet, was of some strange black metal with deep blue sapphires for eyes. The mask was cast in the form of a snarling wolf, with needle-sharp teeth in the open jaws. Standing in the shadows of the hall, his black cloak covering much of his black armour, Baron Meliadus might have been one of the mythical beast-gods that were still worshipped in the lands beyond the Middle Sea. As they entered, he reached up with black-gauntleted hands and removed the mask, revealing a white, heavy face with a well-trimmed black beard and moustache. His hair, too, was black and thick, and his eyes were a pale, strange blue. The baron was apparently unarmed, perhaps as an indication that he came in peace. He bowed low and spoke in a deep, musical voice.

"Greetings, famous Count Brass, and forgive this sudden intrusion. I sent messengers ahead, but they arrived too late to reach you before you left. I am the Baron Meliadus of Kroiden, Grand Constable of the Order of the Wolf, First Chieftain of the Armies under our great King-Emperor Huon . . ."

Count Brass inclined his head. "I know of your great deeds,

Baron Meliadus, and recognized the arms on your carriage. Be welcome. The Castle Brass is yours for as long as you wish to stay. Our fare is simple, I fear, in comparison with the richness I have heard may be sampled at the board of even the lowliest citizen of your mighty empire."

Baron Meliadus smiled. "Your courtliness and hospitality put those of Granbretan to shame, noble hero. I thank you."

Count Brass introduced his daughter, and the baron advanced to bow low and kiss her hand, evidently impressed by her beauty. To Bowgentle he was courteous, showing familiarity with the poet-philosopher's writings, but in reply Bowgentle's voice shook with the effort of remaining polite. With von Villach, Baron Meliadus reminded him of several famous battles in which the old warrior had distinguished himself, and von Villach was visibly pleased.

For all the fine manners and elaborately embellished statements, there was a certain tension in the hall. Bowgentle was the first to make his excuses, and shortly afterward Yisselda and von Villach discreetly left to let Baron Meliadus discuss whatever business had brought him to Castle Brass. Baron Meliadus's eyes lingered just a little while on the girl as she passed out of the hall.

Wine and refreshments were brought, and the two men settled themselves in heavy, carved armchairs.

Baron Meliadus looked over the brim of his wine cup at Count Brass. "You are a man of the world, my lord," he said. "Indeed, you are that in every sense. So you will appreciate that my visit is fostered by more than an urge to enjoy the sights of a pretty province."

Count Brass smiled a little, liking the baron for his frankness. "Quite so," he agreed, "though for my part, it is an honour to meet so famous a servant of the great King Huon."

"That feeling is shared by myself toward you," Baron Meliadus replied. "You are without doubt the most famous hero in Europe, perhaps the most famous in her history. It is almost alarming to find you are made of flesh, after all, and not metal." He laughed, and Count Brass joined in the laughter.

"I've had my share of luck," Count Brass said. "And fate has been kind to me in seeming to corroborate my judgment. Who is to say whether the age we live in is good for me, or I am good for the age?"

"Your philosophy rivals that of your friend Sir Bowgentle," said Baron Meliadus, "and supports what I have heard of your wisdom and judgment. We in Granbretan pride ourselves on our own abilities in that direction, but we could learn from you, I believe."

"I have only details," Count Brass told him, "but you have the talent to see the general scheme." He tried to guess from Meliadus's face what the man was leading toward, but the face remained bland.

"It is the details we need," Baron Meliadus said, "if our general ambitions are to be realized as swiftly as we should like."

Now Count Brass understood why Baron Meliadus was here, but he did not reveal that; he only looked a little puzzled and politely poured more wine for his guest.

"We have a destiny to rule all Europe," Baron Meliadus said.

"That seems to be your destiny," Count Brass agreed. "And I support, in principle, such an ambition."

"I am glad, Count Brass. We are often misrepresented, and our enemies are many, spreading calumnies across the globe."

"I am not interested in the truth or falsehood of those

rumours," Count Brass told him. "It is only your *general* activities I believe in."

"You would not, then, oppose the spread of our empire?" Baron Meliadus looked at him carefully.

"Only," Count Brass smiled, "in particular. In the particular case of this land I protect, Kamarg."

"You would welcome, then, the security of a treaty of peace between us?"

"I see no need for one. I have the security of my towers."

"Hmmm . . ." Baron Meliadus glanced at the floor.

"Is that why you came, my lord Baron? To propose a peace treaty? To propose an alliance, even?"

"Of sorts," nodded the baron. "An alliance of sorts."

"I would not oppose or support you in most senses," Count Brass told him. "I would oppose you only if you attacked my lands. I support you only in my attitude that a unifying force is needed in Europe at this time."

Baron Meliadus thought for a moment before speaking. "And if that unification were threatened?" he said at length.

Count Brass laughed. "I do not believe it can be. There is none powerful enough to withstand Granbretan now."

Baron Meliadus pursed his lips. "You are right in believing that. Our list of victories becomes almost a bore to us. But the more we conquer, the thinner we spread our forces. If we knew the Courts of Europe as well, for instance, as yourself, we should know better who to trust and who to distrust and thus be able to concentrate our attention on the weaknesses. We have the Grand Duke Ziminon as our governor in Normandia, for instance." Baron Meliadus looked carefully at Count Brass. "Would you say we are wise in our choice? He sought the throne of Normandia when his cousin Jewelard possessed it. Is he content with the throne on our terms?"

"Ziminon, eh?" Count Brass smiled. "I helped defeat him at Rouen."

"I know. But what is your opinion of him?"

Count Brass's smile grew broader as Baron Meliadus's manner became more intense. Now he knew exactly what Granbretan wanted of him. "He is an excellent horseman and has a fascination for women," he said.

"That does not help us know the extent to which we may trust him." Almost impatiently, the baron put his wine cup on the table.

"True," Count Brass agreed. He looked up at the large wall clock that hung over the fireplace. Its golden hands showed eleven o'clock. Its huge pendulum swung slowly back and forth, casting a flickering shadow on the wall. It began to strike. "We go to our beds early in Castle Brass," the count said casually. "We live the lives of country folk, I am afraid." He rose from his chair. "I will have a servant show you to your chambers. Your men have been placed in rooms adjoining the main suite."

A faint shadow clouded Baron Meliadus's face. "Count Brass— we know of your skill in politics, your wisdom, your comprehensive knowledge of all the weaknesses and strengths of the European Courts. We wish to make use of that knowledge. In return, we offer riches, power, security . . ."

"I have all I need of the first two and am assured of the third," Count Brass replied gently as he pulled a bellrope. "You will forgive me if I claim tiredness and a desire to sleep. I have had an exerting afternoon."

"Listen to reason, my lord Count, I beg you." Baron Meliadus was making an effort to appear in good temper.

"I hope you will stay with us for some time, Baron, and be able to tell us all the news."

A servant entered.

"Please show our guest to his chambers," Count Brass told the servant. He bowed to the baron. "Good night, Baron Meliadus. I look forward to seeing you when we break our fast at eight o'clock."

When the baron had left the hall following the servant, Count Brass let some of his amusement show on his face. It was pleasing to know that Granbretan sought his help, but he had no intention of giving it. He hoped he could resist the baron's requests politely, for he had no wish to be on bad terms with the Dark Empire. Besides, he quite liked Baron Meliadus. They seemed to share certain beliefs in common.

4

THE FIGHT AT CASTLE BRASS

Baron Meliadus remained at Castle Brass for a week. After the first night, he succeeded in recovering his composure and never again betrayed any sign of impatience with Count Brass for his persistent refusal to listen to the inducements and requirements of Granbretan.

Perhaps it was not only his mission that kept the baron at Castle Brass, for it was plain that he gave Yisselda much of his attention. With her, in particular, he appeared agreeable and courteous to such an extent that it was plain that Yisselda, unfamiliar with the sophisticated ways of the grand courts, was not unattracted to him.

Count Brass seemed oblivious of this. One morning as they walked in the upper terraces of the castle garden, Bowgentle spoke to his friend.

"Baron Meliadus seems not only interested in seducing you for the cause of Granbretan," he said. "He has another kind of seduction in mind, if I'm not mistaken."

"Eh?" Count Brass turned from the contemplation of the vines on the terrace below. "What else is he after?"

"Your daughter," Bowgentle answered softly.

"Come now, Bowgentle!" The count laughed. "You see malice and evil intention in the man's every action. He is a gentleman, a noble. And besides, he wants something from me. He would not let the ambition be jeopardized by a flirtation. I think you do Baron Meliadus an injustice. I've grown rather to like him."

"Then it is high time you involved yourself in politics again, my lord," said Bowgentle with some fire, but all the time speaking softly, "for it would seem your judgment is not as sharp as it was!"

Count Brass shrugged. "Be that as it may, I think you are becoming a nervous old woman, my friend. Baron Meliadus has behaved with decorum since his arrival. Admittedly, I think he wastes his time here and wish he would decide to leave soon, but if he has intentions toward my daughter I have seen no sign of it. He might wish to marry her, certainly, in order to make a blood tie between myself and Granbretan, but Yisselda would not consent to the idea, and neither would I."

"What if Yisselda loved Baron Meliadus and he felt passion for her?"

"How could she love Baron Meliadus?"

"She sees few men as handsome and sophisticated in Kamarg."

"Hmm," grunted the count dismissively. "If she loved the

baron, she'd tell me, wouldn't she? I'll believe your tale when I hear it confirmed from Yisselda's lips!"

Bowgentle wondered to himself if the count's refusal to see the truth were sponsored by a secret wish to know nothing at all of the character of those who ruled Granbretan or whether it was simply a father's common inability to see in his child what was perfectly evident to others. Bowgentle decided to keep a careful eye on both Baron Meliadus and Yisselda in future. He could not believe that the count's judgment was correct in the case of the man who had caused the Massacre of Liège, who had given the order for the Sack of Sahbruck, and whose perverse appetites were the horror of every whispering scullion from North Cape to Tunis. As he had said, the count had lived too long in the country, breathing the clean rural air. Now he could not recognize the stink of corruption even when he smelled it.

Though Count Brass was reticent in his conversations with Baron Meliadus, the Granbretanian seemed willing to tell him much. It appeared that even where Granbretan did not rule, there were discontented nobles and peasants willing to make secret treaties with the agents of the Dark Empire, in promise of power under the King-Emperor if they helped destroy those who opposed Granbretan. And Granbretan's ambitions, it seemed, extended even into Asia. Beyond the Mediterranean there were well-established groups ready to support the Dark Empire when the time came for attack. Count Brass's admiration for the tactical skills of the empire increased every day.

"Within twenty years," said Baron Meliadus, "the whole of Europe will be ours. Within thirty, all Arabia and the countries that surround it. Within fifty, we shall have the strength to attack that mysterious land on our maps that is called Asiacommunista . . ."

"An ancient and romantic name," smiled Count Brass, "full of great sorceries, it's said. Is that not where the Runestaff lies?"

"Aye, that's the tale—that it stands on the tallest mountain in the world, where snow swirls and winds howl constantly, protected by hairy men of incredible wisdom and age, who are ten feet high and have the faces of apes." Baron Meliadus smiled. "But there are many places that the Runestaff is said to be—in Amarehk, even."

Count Brass nodded. "Ah, Amarehk—do you include that land in your dreams of empire?" Amarehk was the great continent said to lie across the water to the west, ruled by beings of almost godlike powers. They were reputed to lead lives that were abstracted, tranquil, and remote. Theirs, so the tales went, was the civilization that altogether missed the effects of the Tragic Millennium, when the rest of the world collapsed into various degrees of ruin. Count Brass had jested when he mentioned Amarehk, but Baron Meliadus looked at him sidewise, a gleam in his pale eye.

"Why not?" he said. "I would storm the walls of heaven if I found them."

Disturbed, Count Brass left him shortly thereafter, for the first time wondering if his resolution to remain neutral were as well advised as he'd believed.

Yisselda, though as intelligent as her father, lacked both his experience and his normally good judgment of character. She found even the baron's infamous reputation attractive and at the same time could not believe that all the stories about him were true. For when he spoke to her in his soft, cultivated voice, flattering her beauty and grace, she thought she saw a man of gentle temperament forced to appear grim and ruthless by the conventions of his office and his role in history.

Now, for the third time since his arrival, she slipped at night from her bedchamber to keep an assignation with him in the west tower, which had been unused since the bloody death there of the previous Lord Guardian.

The meetings had been innocent enough—a clasping of her hand, a brushing of her lips with his, the whispering of love words, talk of marriage. Though still unsure of the latter suggestion (for she loved her father and felt it would hurt him deeply if she married Baron Meliadus), she could not resist the attention the baron gave her. Even she was not sure that it was love she felt for him, but she welcomed the sense of adventure and excitement that these meetings gave her.

On this particular night, as she sped light-footed through the gloomy corridors, she did not know that she was being followed. Behind her came a figure in a black cloak, a long dagger in a leather sheath in its right hand.

Heart beating, red lips parted slightly in a half smile, Yisselda ran up the winding steps of the tower until she came to the little turret room where the baron already awaited her.

He bowed low, then caught her in his arms, caressing her soft flesh through the thin, silken nightgown she wore. His kiss was firmer this time, almost brutal, and her breathing became deeper as she returned it, clutching at his broad, leather-clad back. Now his hand moved down to her waist, and then to her thigh, and for a moment she pressed her body closer to his and then tried to tug away as she felt a growing, unfamiliar panic.

He held on to her, panting. A beam of moonlight entered the narrow window and fell across his face, revealing frowning brows and heated eyes.

"Yisselda, you must marry me. Tonight we can leave Castle Brass and be beyond the towers by tomorrow. Your father would not dare follow us to Granbretan."

"My father would dare anything," she said with quiet conviction, "but I feel, my lord, that I have no wish to put him to the trouble."

"What do you mean?"

"I mean that I would not marry without his consent."

"Would he give it?"

"I believe not."

"Then . . ."

She tried to tug away completely from him, but his strong hands gripped her arms. Now she was frightened, wondering how her former passion could turn so swiftly into fear. "I must go now."

"No! Yisselda, I am not used to my will being opposed. First your obstinate father refuses what I ask—now you! I'd kill you rather than let you leave without promising to come with me to Granbretan!" He pulled her toward him, his lips forcing a kiss from her. She moaned as she tried to resist.

Then the dark, cloaked figure entered the chamber, unsheathing the long dagger from its case. The steel shone in the moonlight, and Baron Meliadus glared at the intruder but did not relinquish his hold on the girl.

"Let her go," said the dark figure, "for if you do not I'll forsake all principle and slay you now."

"Bowgentle!" Yisselda sobbed. "Run for my father—you are not strong enough to fight him!"

Baron Meliadus laughed and threw Yisselda to the corner of the turret room. "Fight? It would not be a fight with you, philosopher—it would be butchery. Stand aside and I'll leave—but I must take the girl."

"Leave alone," Bowgentle replied. "By all means do that, for I have no wish to have your death on my conscience. But Yisselda stays with me."

"She's leaving with me tonight—whether she wills it or no!" Meliadus flung back his own cloak, revealing a short sword high at his waist. "Aside, Sir Bowgentle, for unless you move, I promise that you will not live to write a sonnet about *this* affair!"

Bowgentle stood his ground, dagger held point outward at Baron Meliadus's chest.

The Granbretanian's hand gripped the hilt of the sword and drew it from the scabbard in a blur of movement.

"One last chance, philosopher!"

Bowgentle did not reply. His half-glazed eyes did not blink. Only the hand holding the dagger shook slightly.

Yisselda screamed. The scream was high-pitched and penetrating, echoing through the castle.

Baron Meliadus turned with a grunt of rage, raising the sword.

Bowgentle leaped forward, stabbing clumsily with the dagger, which was deflected by the tough leather the baron wore. Meliadus turned with a laugh of contempt, his sword struck twice at Bowgentle, once at his head and once at his body, and the

philosopher-poet fell to the flagstones, his blood staining the floor. Again Yisselda screamed, this time in terror and pity for her father's friend. Baron Meliadus stooped and grabbed the struggling girl by her arm, twisted it so that she gasped, and flung her over his shoulder. Then he left the turret room and began to descend the steps swiftly.

He had to cross the main hall to get to his own quarters, and as he entered it, there came a roar from the other side. By the light of the dying fire he saw Count Brass, clad only in a loose robe, his great broadsword in his hands, blocking the door through which Baron Meliadus meant to go.

"Father!" Yisselda cried, and then the Granbretanian had flung her to one side and brandished his short sword at Count Brass.

"So Bowgentle was right," Count Brass rumbled. "You abuse my hospitality, Baron."

"I want your daughter. She loves me."

"So it seems." Count Brass glanced at Yisselda as she climbed to her feet, sobbing. "Defend yourself, Baron."

Baron Meliadus frowned. "You have a broadsword—my blade's little better than a bodkin. Besides, I've no wish to fight a man of your years. We can make peace, surely . . ."

"Father—he has killed Bowgentle!"

Count Brass trembled with rage at this. He strode to the wall where a rack of swords was placed, took the largest and best balanced from the rack, and flung it to Baron Meliadus. It clattered on the flagstones. Meliadus dropped his own blade and picked up the broadsword. Now he had the advantage, for he wore stout leather and the count wore only linen.

Count Brass advanced, the broadsword raised, then swung at

Baron Meliadus, who met the swipe with a parry. Like men hewing at a great tree, they swung the heavy blades this way and that. The clangour rang through the hall and brought servants scurrying, as well as the baron's men-at-arms, who looked disconcerted and uncertain what to do. By that time, von Villach and his men had arrived; the Granbretanians saw that they were heavily outnumbered and decided to do nothing.

Sparks scattered into the darkness of the hall as the two big men dueled, the broadswords rising and falling, swinging this way and that, every stroke parried with masterly skill. Sweat covered both faces as the swords swung; both chests heaved with the exertion as they fenced back and forth across the hall.

Now Baron Meliadus cut at Count Brass's shoulder but succeeded only in grazing it. Next Count Brass's sword fell on Baron Meliadus's side but was blocked by the thick leather of the baron's doublet. There was a series of swift strokes in which it seemed both men must be cut to pieces, but when they stepped back and resumed their guard all Count Brass had was a light cut across his forehead and a tear in his gown, and Baron Meliadus's coat was ripped down the front and one arm of it hung in tatters.

The sound of their panting and the scrape of their feet on the floor blended with the great clash of blades as they met again and again.

Then Count Brass tripped over a small table and fell backward, legs sprawling, one hand losing its grip on the sword. Baron Meliadus smirked and raised his weapon; Count Brass rolled over, swiped at the baron's legs, brought the man thumping down beside him.

The blades forgotten for the moment, they wrestled over and

over on the flagstones, fists battering at one another, lips snarling, swords still attached to them by wrist thongs.

Then Baron Meliadus flung himself backward and jumped up, but Count Brass was up again too. He swung his sword suddenly and knocked the baron's blade with such force that the thong snapped and the sword sailed clear across the hall, where it stuck point first in a wooden pillar and thrummed like a metal organ reed.

Count Brass's eyes showed no pity. They held only an intention to kill Baron Meliadus.

"You slew my true and greatest friend," he growled as he raised his broadsword. Baron Meliadus slowly folded his arms across his chest and waited for the blow, eyes downcast, an almost bored expression on his face.

"You slew Bowgentle, and for that I slay you."

"Count Brass!"

The count hesitated, the sword raised above his head.

The voice was Bowgentle's.

"Count Brass, he did not kill me. The flat of his sword stunned me, and the wound in my chest is by no means mortal." Bowgentle came forward through the crowd, his hand on his wound, a livid bruise on his forehead.

Count Brass sighed. "Thank fate for that, Bowgentle. Nonetheless . . ." He turned to contemplate Baron Meliadus. "This villain has abused my hospitality, insulted my daughter, injured my friend . . ."

Baron Meliadus raised his eyes to meet the count's. "Forgive me, Count Brass. Moved by a passion for the beauty of Yisselda as I was, it clouded my brain, possessed me like a demon. I would not beg when you threatened my life, but now I ask you to understand that only honest, human emotions moved me to do what I did."

Count Brass shook his head. "I cannot forgive you, Baron. I'll listen to your insidious words no longer. You must be gone from Castle Brass within the hour and off my lands by morning, or you and yours will perish."

"You'd risk offending Granbretan?"

Count Brass shrugged. "I do not offend the Dark Empire. If they hear anything like the truth of what passed this night, they will punish you for your mistakes, not come against me for having seen justice done. You have failed in your mission. *You* have offended *me*—not I, Granbretan."

Baron Meliadus said no more but, fuming, left to prepare himself for his journey. Disgraced and enraged, he was soon in his bizarre carriage, and the carriage was rolling through the castle gates before half an hour had passed. He made no farewells.

Count Brass, Yisselda, Bowgentle, and von Villach stood in the courtyard watching him leave.

"You were right, Bowgentle," muttered the count. "Both Yisselda and I were beguiled by the man. I'll have no more emissaries from Granbretan visit Castle Brass."

"You realize that the Dark Empire must be fought, destroyed?" Bowgentle asked hopefully.

"I did not say that. Let it do what it will. *We* will have no further trouble from Granbretan or Baron Meliadus."

"You are wrong," Bowgentle said with conviction.

———

And in his dark carriage, as it bumped through the night toward the northern borders of Kamarg, Baron Meliadus spoke aloud to himself and swore an oath by the most mysterious and sacred object he knew. He swore by the Runestaff (that lost artifact said to contain all the secrets of destiny) that he would get Count Brass into his power by any means possible, that he would possess Yisselda, and that Kamarg would become one great furnace in which all who inhabited it would perish.

This he swore by the Runestaff, and thus the destiny of Baron Meliadus, Count Brass, Yisselda, the Dark Empire, and all who were now and would be later concerned with the events in Castle Brass was irrevocably decided.

The play was cast, the stage set, the curtain raised.

Now the mummers must enact their destiny.

BOOK TWO

Those who dare swear by the Runestaff must then benefit or suffer from the consequences of the fixed pattern of destiny that they set in motion. Some several such oaths have been sworn in the history of the Runestaff's existence, but none with such vast and terrible results as the mighty oath of vengeance sworn by the Baron Meliadus of Kroiden the year before that aspect of the Champion Eternal, Dorian Hawkmoon von Köln, entered into the pages of this ancient narrative.

—*The High History of the Runestaff*

1

DORIAN HAWKMOON

Baron Meliadus returned to Londra, gloomy-towered capital of the Dark Empire, and brooded for almost a year before he settled on his plan. Other affairs of Granbretan occupied him in that time. There were rebellions to put down, examples to be made of newly conquered towns, fresh battles to be planned and fought, puppet governors to be interviewed and placed in power.

Baron Meliadus fulfilled all these responsibilities faithfully and with imagination, but his passion for Yisselda and his hatred of Count Brass were never far from his thoughts. Although he had suffered no ignominy for his failure to win the count to Granbretan's cause, he still felt thwarted. Besides, he was constantly finding problems in which the count could have helped him easily. Whenever such a problem arose, Baron Meliadus's brain became clogged with a dozen different schemes of revenge, but none seemed suited to do everything he required. He must have Yisselda, he must get the count's aid in the affairs of Europe, he must destroy Kamarg as he had sworn. They were incompatible ambitions.

In his tall tower of obsidian, overlooking the blood-red River Tayme where barges of bronze and ebony carried cargo from the coast, Baron Meliadus paced his cluttered study with its tapestries of time-faded browns, blacks, and blues, its orreries of precious metal and gemstones, its globes and astrolabes of beaten iron and brass and silver, its furniture of dark, polished wood, and its carpets of deep pile the colours of leaves in autumn.

Around him, on all the walls, on every shelf, in every angle, were his clocks. All were in perfect synchronization, and all struck on the quarter, half, and full hour, many with musical effects. They were of various shapes and sizes, in cases of metal, wood, or certain other, less recognizable substances. They were ornately carved, to the extent, sometimes, that it was virtually impossible to tell the time from them. They had been collected from many parts of Europe and the Near East, the spoils of a score of conquered provinces. They were what Baron Meliadus loved most among his many possessions. Not only this study, but every room in the great tower, was full of clocks. There was a huge four-faced clock in bronze, onyx, gold, silver, and platinum at the very top of the tower, and when its great bells were struck by life-size figures of naked girls holding hammers, all Londra echoed with the din. The clocks rivaled in variety those of Meliadus's brother-in-law, Taragorm, Master of the Palace of Time, whom Meliadus loathed with a deep attachment as rival for his strange sister's perverse and whimful affections.

Baron Meliadus ceased his pacing and picked up a piece of parchment from his desk. It contained the latest information from the province of Köln, a province that, nearly two years previously, Meliadus had made an example of. It seemed now that too much had been done, for the son of the old Duke of Köln (whom Meliadus had personally disemboweled in the public square of the capital) had raised an army of rebellion and almost succeeded in crushing the occupying forces of Granbretan. Had not speedy reinforcements, in the shape of ornithopters armed with long-range flame-lances, been sent, Köln might have been temporarily taken from the Dark Empire.

But the ornithopters had demolished the forces of the young duke, and he had been made prisoner. He was due soon to arrive in Londra to pleasure the nobles of Granbretan with his sufferings. Here again was a situation where Count Brass might have helped, for before he showed himself in open rebellion, the Duke of Köln had offered himself as a mercenary commander to the Dark Empire and had been accepted, had fought well in the service of Granbretan, at Nürnberg and Ulm, winning the confidence of the Empire, gaining command of a force comprised mainly of soldiers who had once served his father, then turning with them and marching back to Köln to attack the province.

Baron Meliadus frowned, for the young duke had provided an example that others might now follow. Already he was a hero in the German provinces, by all accounts. Few dared oppose the Dark Empire as he had done.

If only Count Brass had agreed . . .

Suddenly Baron Meliadus began to smile, a scheme seeming to spring instantly and complete into his mind. Perhaps the young

Duke of Köln could be used in some way, other than in the entertainment of his peers.

Baron Meliadus put down the parchment and pulled at a bell-rope. A girl-slave entered, her naked body rouged all over, and fell on her knees to receive his instructions. (All the baron's slaves were female; he allowed no men into his tower for fear of treachery.) "Take a message to the master of the prison catacombs," he told the girl. "Tell him that Baron Meliadus would interview the prisoner Dorian Hawkmoon von Köln as soon as he arrives there."

"Yes, master." The girl rose and backed from the room, leaving Baron Meliadus staring from his window at the river, a faint smile on his full lips.

Dorian Hawkmoon, bound in chains of gilded iron (as befitted his station in the eyes of the Granbretanians), stumbled down the gangplank from barge to quay, blinking in the evening light and staring around him at the huge, menacing towers of Londra. If he had never before needed proof of the congenital insanity of the inhabitants of the Dark Island, he had, to his mind, full evidence now. There was something unnatural about every line of the architecture, every choice of colour and carving. And yet there was also a sense of great strength about it, of purpose and intelligence. No wonder, he thought, it was hard to fathom the psychology of the people of the Dark Empire, when so much of them was paradox.

A guard, in white leather and wearing the white metal death's-head mask that was uniform to the Order he served, pushed him gently forward. Hawkmoon staggered in spite of the lightness of the pressure, for he had not eaten for almost a week. His brain was at once clouded and abstracted; he was hardly aware of the significance of his circumstances. Since his capture at the Battle of Köln, no-one had spoken to him. He had lain most of the time in the darkness of the ship's bilges, drinking occasionally from the trough of dirty water that had been fixed beside him. He was unshaven, his eyes were glazed, his long, fair hair was matted, and his torn mail and breeches were covered in filth. The chains had chafed his skin so that red sores were prominent on his neck and wrists, but he felt no pain. Indeed, he felt little of anything, moved like a sleepwalker, saw everything as if in a dream.

He took two steps along the quartz quay, staggered, and fell to one knee. The guards, now on either side of him, pulled him up and supported him as he approached a black wall that loomed over the quay. There was a small barred door in the wall, and two soldiers, in ruby-coloured pig masks, stood on either side of it. The Order of the Pig controlled the prisons of Londra. The guards spoke a few words to each other in the grunting secret language of their Order, and one of them laughed, grabbing Hawkmoon's arm, saying nothing to the prisoner but pushing him forward as the other guard swung the barred door inward.

The interior was dark. The door closed behind Hawkmoon, and for a few moments he was alone. Then, in the dim light from the door, he saw a mask; a pig mask, but more elaborate than those of the guards outside. Another similar mask appeared, and then another. Hawkmoon was seized and led through the foul-smelling darkness, led down into the prison catacombs of the Dark Empire, knowing, with little emotion, that his life was over.

At last he heard another door open. He was pushed into a tiny chamber; then he heard the door close and a beam fall into place.

The air in the dungeon was foetid, and there was a film of foulness on the flagstones and wall. Hawkmoon lay against the wall and then slid gradually to the floor. Whether he fainted or fell asleep, he could not tell, but his eyes closed and oblivion came.

A week before, he had been the Hero of Köln, a champion against the aggressors, a man of grace and sardonic wit, a warrior of skill. Now, as a matter of course, the men of Granbretan had turned him into an animal—an animal with little will to live. A lesser man might have clung grimly to his humanity, fed from his hatred, schemed escape; but Hawkmoon, having lost all, wanted nothing.

Perhaps he would awake from his trance. If he did, he would be a different man from the one who had fought with such insolent courage at the Battle of Köln.

2

THE BARGAIN

Torchlight and the glinting of beast-masks; sneering pig and snarling wolf, red metal and black; mocking eyes, diamond white and sapphire blue. The heavy rustle of cloaks and the sound of whispered conversation.

Hawkmoon sighed weakly and closed his eyes, then opened them again as footsteps came nearer and the wolf bent over him, holding the torch close to his face. The heat was uncomfortable, but Hawkmoon made no effort to move away from it.

Wolf straightened and spoke to pig.

"Pointless speaking to him now. Feed him, wash him. Restore his intelligence a little."

Pig and wolf left, closing the door. Hawkmoon closed his eyes.

When he next awoke, he was being carried through corridors

by the light of brands. He was taken into a room lighted by lamps. There was a bed covered in rich furs and silks, food laid out on a carved table, a bath of some shimmering orange metal, full of steaming water, two girl-slaves in attendance.

The chains were stripped from him, then the clothes; then he was picked up again and lowered into the water. It stung his skin as the slaves began to lave him, while a man entered with a razor and began to trim his hair and shave his beard. All this Hawkmoon took passively, staring at the mosaic ceiling with blank eyes. He allowed himself to be dressed in fine, soft linen, with a shirt of silk and breeches of velvet, and gradually, a dim feeling of well-being overcame him. But when they first sat him at the table and pushed fruit into his mouth, his stomach contracted and he retched. So they gave him a little drugged milk, then put him on the bed and left him, save for one slave at the door, watching over him.

Some days passed, and gradually Hawkmoon began to eat, began to appreciate the luxury of his existence. There were books in the room, and the women were his, but he still had little inclination to sample either.

Hawkmoon, whose mind had gone to sleep so soon after his capture, took a long time to awaken, and when at length he did, it was to remember his past life as a dream. He opened a book one day, and the letters looked strange, though he could read them well enough. It was simply that he saw no point in them, no importance in the words and sentences they formed, though the book had been written by a scholar once his favourite philosopher. He shrugged and dropped the book onto a table. One of the girl-slaves, seeing this action, pressed herself against his body and stroked his cheek. Gently, he pushed her aside and went to the bed, lying down with his hands behind his head.

At length, he said, "Why am I here?"

They were the first words he had spoken.

"Oh, my lord Duke, I know not—save that you seem an honoured prisoner."

"A game, I suppose, before the Lords of Granbretan have their sport with me?" Hawkmoon spoke without emotion. His voice was flat but deep. Even the words seemed strange to him as he spoke them. He looked out from his inward-turned eyes at the girl, and she trembled. She had long, blond hair and was well-shaped; a girl from Scandia by her accent.

"I know nothing, my lord, only that I must please you in any way you desire."

Hawkmoon nodded slightly and glanced about the room. "They prepare me for some torture or display, I would guess," he said to himself.

The room had no windows, but by the quality of the air Hawkmoon judged that they were still underground, probably in the prison catacombs somewhere. He measured the passing of time by the lamps; they seemed to be filled about once a day. He stayed in the room for a fortnight or so before he again saw the wolf who had visited him in his cell.

The door opened without ceremony, and in stepped the tall figure, dressed in black leather from head to foot, with a long sword (black-hilted) in a black leather scabbard. The black wolf mask hid the whole head. From it issued the rich, musical voice he had only half-heard before.

"So, our prisoner seems restored to his former wit and fitness."

The two girl-slaves bowed and withdrew. Hawkmoon rose from the bed on which he had lain most of the time since his arrival. He swung his body off the bed and got to his feet.

"Good. Quite fit, Duke von Köln?"

"Aye." Hawkmoon's voice contained no inflection. He yawned unselfconsciously, decided there was little point in standing after all, and resumed his former position on the bed.

"I take it that you know me," said the wolf, a hint of impatience in his voice.

"No."

"You have not guessed?"

Hawkmoon made no reply.

The wolf moved across the room and stood by the table, which had a huge crystal bowl of fruit on it. His gloved hand picked up a pomegranate, and the wolf-mask bent as if inspecting it. "You *are* fully recovered, my lord?"

"It would seem so," answered Hawkmoon. "I have a great sense of well-being. All my needs are attended to, as, I believe, you ordered. And now, I presume, you intend to make some sport with me?"

"That does not seem to disturb you."

Hawkmoon shrugged. "It will end eventually."

"It could last a lifetime. We of Granbretan are inventive."

"A lifetime is not so long."

"As it happens," the wolf told him, tossing the fruit from hand to hand, "we were thinking of sparing you the discomfort."

Hawkmoon's face showed no expression.

"You are very self-contained, my lord Duke," the wolf continued. "Strangely so, since you live only because of the whim of

your enemies—those same enemies who slew your father so dis-
gracefully."

Hawkmoon's brows contracted as if in faint recollection. "I remember that," he said vaguely. "My father. The old Duke."

The wolf threw the pomegranate to the floor and raised the
mask. The handsome, black-bearded features were revealed. "It
was I, Baron Meliadus of Kroiden, who slew him." There was a
goading smile on the full lips.

"Baron Meliadus . . . ? Ah . . . who slew him?"

"All the manliness has gone from you, my lord," Baron
Meliadus murmured. "Or do you seek to deceive us in the hope
that you may turn traitor upon us again?"

Hawkmoon pursed his lips. "I am tired," he said.

Meliadus's eyes were puzzled and almost angry. "I killed your
father!"

"So you said."

"Well!" Disconcerted, Meliadus turned away and paced toward the door, then wheeled around again. "That is not what
I came here to discuss. It seems, however, strange that you should
profess no hatred or wish for vengeance against me."

Hawkmoon himself began to feel bored, wishing that Meliadus
would leave him in peace. The man's tense manner and his half-
hysterical expressions discomfited him rather as the buzzing of a
mosquito could be distracting to a man wishing to sleep.

"I feel nothing," Hawkmoon replied, hoping that this would
satisfy the intruder.

"You have no spirit left!" Meliadus exclaimed angrily. "No
spirit! Defeat and capture have robbed you of it!"

"Perhaps. Now, I am tired . . ."

"I came to offer you the return of your lands," Meliadus went on. "An entirely autonomous state within our empire. More than we have ever offered a conquered land before."

Now just a trace of curiosity stirred in Hawkmoon. "Why is that?" he said.

"We wish to strike a bargain with you—to our mutual benefit. We need a man who is crafty and war skilled, as you are"— Baron Meliadus frowned in doubt—"or seemed to be. And we need someone who would be trusted by those who do not trust Granbretan." This was not at all the way Meliadus had intended to present the bargain, but Hawkmoon's strange lack of emotion had disconcerted him. "We wish you to perform an errand for us. In return—your lands."

"I would like to go home," Hawkmoon nodded. "The mead-ows of my childhood . . ." He smiled in reminiscence.

Shocked by a display of what he mistook for sentimentality, Baron Meliadus snapped, "What you do when you return— whether you make daisy chains or build castles—is of no interest to us. You will return, however, only if you perform your mission faithfully."

Hawkmoon's introverted eyes glanced up at Meliadus. "You think I have lost my reason, perhaps, my lord?"

"I'm not sure. We have means of discovering that. Our sorcerer-scientists will make certain tests . . ."

"I am sane, Baron Meliadus. Saner, maybe, than I ever was. You have nothing to fear from me."

Baron Meliadus raised his eyes to the ceiling. "By the Runestaff, will no-one take sides?" He opened the door. "We will find out about *you*, Duke von Köln. You will be sent for later today!"

After Baron Meliadus had left, Hawkmoon continued to lie on the bed. The interview was quickly gone from his mind and only half-remembered when, in two or three hours, pig-masked guards entered the chamber and told him to accompany them.

Hawkmoon was led through many passages, marching steadily upward until they reached a great iron door. One of the guards banged on it with the butt of his flame-lance, and it creaked open to admit fresh air and daylight. Waiting beyond the door was a detachment of guards in purple armour and cloaks, with the purple masks of the Order of the Bull covering their faces. Hawkmoon was handed over to them and, looking about him, saw that he stood in a wide courtyard that but for a gravel path was covered by a fine lawn. A high wall, in which was set a narrow gate, surrounded the lawn, and on it paced guards of the Order of the Pig. Behind the wall jutted the gloomy towers of the city.

Hawkmoon was guided along the path to the gate, through the gate, and into a narrow street where a carriage of gilded ebony, fashioned in the shape of a two-headed horse, awaited him. Into this he climbed, accompanied by two silent guards. The carriage began to move. Through a chink in its curtains, Hawkmoon saw the towers as they passed. It was sunset, and a lurid light suffused the city.

Eventually the carriage stopped. Hawkmoon passively allowed the guards to lead him out of it and saw at once that he had come to the palace of the King-Emperor Huon.

The palace rose, tier upon tier, almost out of sight. Four great towers surmounted it, and these towers glowed with a deep golden light. The palace was decorated with bas-reliefs depicting strange rites, battle scenes, famous episodes in Granbretan's long history,

gargoyles, figurines, abstract shapes—the whole a grotesque and fantastic structure that had been built over centuries. Every kind of building material had been used in its construction and then coloured, so that the building shone with a mixture of shades covering the entire spectrum. And there was no order to the placing of the colour, no attempt to match or contrast. One colour flowed into the next, straining the eye, offending the brain. The palace of a madman, overshadowing, in its impression of insanity, the rest of the city.

At its gates yet another set of guards awaited Hawkmoon. These were garbed in the masks and armour of the Order of the Mantis, the Order to which King Huon himself belonged. Their elaborate insect masks were covered in jewels, with antennae of platinum wire and eyes faceted with a score or more of different gemstones. The men had long, thin legs and arms and slender bodies encased in insectlike plate armour of black, gold, and green. When they spoke their secret language to each other, it was the rustle and click of insect voices.

For the first time, Hawkmoon felt disturbed as these guards led him into the lower passages of the palace, the walls of which were of deep scarlet metal that reflected distorted images as they moved.

At last they entered a large, high-ceilinged hall whose dark walls were veined, like marble, with white, green, and pink. But these veins moved constantly, flickering and changing course the length and breadth of the walls and ceiling.

The floor of the hall, which was the best part of a quarter of a mile long and almost as wide, was filled at intervals by devices that Hawkmoon took to be machines of some description, though he could not understand their function. Like everything he had seen since arriving in Londra, these machines were ornate, much decorated, built from precious metals and semiprecious stones. There were instruments set into them unlike anything he knew, and many of the instruments were active, registering, counting, measuring, tended by men who wore the serpent masks of the Order of the Snake—the Order that consisted solely of sorcerers and scientists in the service of the King-Emperor. They were shrouded in mottled cloaks with cowls half-drawn over their heads.

Down the central aisle a figure paced toward Hawkmoon, waving to the guards to dismiss.

Hawkmoon judged this man high in the Order, for his serpent mask was much more ornate than those of the others. He might even be the Grand Constable, by his bearing and general demeanour.

"My lord Duke, greetings."

Hawkmoon acknowledged the bow with a slight one of his own, many of the habits of his former life still being with him.

"I am Baron Kalan of Vitall, Chief Scientist to the King-Emperor. You are to be my guest for a day or so, I understand. Welcome to my apartments and laboratories."

"Thank you. What do you wish me to do?" Hawkmoon asked abstractedly.

"First, I hope you will dine with me."

Baron Kalan signaled graciously for Hawkmoon to precede him, and they walked the length of the hall, passing many peculiar constructions, until they arrived at a door that led to what were obviously the baron's private apartments. A meal was already

laid. It was comparatively simple, judged against what Hawkmoon had been eating over the past fortnight, but it was well
cooked and tasty. When they had finished, Baron Kalan, who
had already removed his mask to reveal a pale, middle-aged face
with a wispy white beard and thinning hair, poured wine for
them both. They had scarcely spoken during the meal.

Hawkmoon tasted the wine. It was excellent.

"My own invention, the wine," said Kalan, and smirked.

"It is unfamiliar," Hawkmoon admitted. "What grape . . . ?"

"No grape—but grain. A somewhat different process."

"It is strong."

"Stronger than most wines," agreed the baron. "Now, Duke,
you know that I have been commissioned to establish your sanity,
judge your temperament, and decide whether you are fit to serve
His Majesty the King-Emperor Huon."

"I believe that is what Baron Meliadus told me." Hawkmoon
smiled faintly. "I will be interested in learning your observations."

"Hmm . . ." Baron Kalan looked closely at Hawkmoon. "I can
see why I was asked to entertain you. I must say that you *appear*
to be rational."

"Thank you." Under the influence of the strange wine, Hawkmoon was rediscovering some of his former irony.

Baron Kalan rubbed at his face and coughed a dry, barely heard
cough for some several moments. His manner had contained a
certain nervousness since he removed the mask. Hawkmoon had
already noticed how the people of Granbretan preferred to keep
their masks on most of the time. Now Kalan reached toward the
extravagant snake mask and placed it over his head. The coughing
stopped immediately, and the man's body relaxed visibly. Although

Hawkmoon had heard that it was a breach of Granbretanian etiquette to retain one's mask when entertaining a guest of noble station, he affected to show no surprise at the baron's action.

"Ah, my lord Duke," came the whisper from within the mask, "who am I to judge what sanity is? There are those who judge us of Granbretan insane . . ."

"Surely not."

"It is true. Those with blunted perceptions, who cannot see the grand plan, are not convinced of the nobility of our great crusade. They say, you know, that *we* are mad, ha, ha!" Baron Kalan rose. "But now, if you will accompany me, we will begin our preliminary investigations."

Back through the hall of machines they went, entering another hall, only slightly smaller than the first. This had the same dark walls, but these pulsed with an energy that gradually shifted along the spectrum from violet to black and back again. There was only a single machine in the hall, a thing of gleaming blue-and-red metal, with projections, arms, and attachments, a great bell-like object suspended from an intricate scaffold affair that was part of the machine. On one side was a console, attended by a dozen men in the uniform of the Order of the Snake, their metal masks partially reflecting the pulsing light from the walls. A noise filled the hall, emanating from the machine, a faintly heard clatter, a moan, a series of hissings as if it breathed like a beast.

"This is our mentality machine," Baron Kalan said proudly. "This is what will test you."

"It is very large," said Hawkmoon, stepping toward it.

"One of our largest. It has to be. It must perform complex tasks. This is the result of *scientific* sorcery, my lord Duke, none of your hit-and-miss spell singing you find on the Continent. It is our science that gives us our chief advantage over lesser nations."

As the effect of the drink wore off, Hawkmoon became increasingly the man he had been in the prison catacombs. His sense of detachment grew, and when he was led forward and made to stand under the bell when it was lowered, he felt little anxiety or curiosity.

At last the bell completely covered him, and its fleshy sides moved in to mould themselves around his body. It was an obscene embrace and would have horrified the Dorian Hawkmoon who had fought the Battle of Köln, but this new Hawkmoon felt only a vague impatience and discomfort. He began to feel a crawling sensation in his skull, as if incredibly fine wires were entering his head and probing at his brain. Hallucinations began to manifest themselves. He saw bright oceans of colour, distorted faces, buildings and flora of unnatural perspective. It rained jewels for a hundred years, and then black winds blew across his eyes and were torn apart to reveal oceans that were at once frozen and in motion, beasts of infinite sympathy and goodness, women of monstrous tenderness. Interspersed with these visions came clear memories of his childhood, of his life up until the moment he had entered the machine. Piece by piece, the memories built up until the whole of his life had been recalled and presented to him. But still he felt no other emotion save the remembrance of the emotion he had had in that past time. When at last the sides of the bell moved back and the bell itself began to rise, Hawkmoon stood impassively, feeling as if he had witnessed the experience of another.

Kalan was there and took his arm, leading him away from the mentality machine. "The preliminary investigations show you to be rather more than normally sane, my lord Duke—if I read the instruments correctly. The mentality machine will report in detail in a few hours. Now you must rest, and we shall continue our tests in the morning."

The next day Hawkmoon was again given over to the embrace of the mentality machine, and this time he lay full-length within its belly, looking upward while picture after picture was flashed before his eyes and the pictures that they first reminded him of were then flashed onto a screen. Hawkmoon's face hardly altered its expression while all this went on. He experienced a series of hallucinations where he was thrown into highly dangerous situations—an ocean ghoul attacking him, an avalanche, three swordsmen as opponents, the need to leap from the third storey of a building or be burned to death—and in every case he rescued himself with courage and skill, though his reflexes were mechanical, uninspired by any particular sense of fear. Many such tests were made, and he passed through them all without ever once showing any strong emotion of any kind. Even when he was induced by the mentality machine to laugh, weep, hate, love, and so on, the reactions were chiefly physical in expression.

At length Hawkmoon was released by the machine and faced Baron Kalan's snake mask.

"It would seem that you are, in some peculiar way, *too* sane, my lord Duke," whispered the baron. "A paradox, eh? Aye, too sane. It is as if some part of your brain has disappeared altogether or has been cut off from the rest. However, I can only report to Baron Meliadus that you seem eminently suited to his purpose, so long as certain sensible precautions are taken."

"What purpose is that?" Hawkmoon asked with no real interest.

"That is for him to say."

Shortly afterward, Baron Kalan took his leave of Hawkmoon, who was escorted through a labyrinth of corridors by two guards of the Order of the Mantis. At length they arrived outside a door of burnished silver that opened to reveal a sparsely furnished room entirely lined with mirrors on walls, floor, and ceiling, save for a single large window at the far end that opened onto a balcony overlooking the city. Near the window stood a figure in a black wolf mask who could only be Baron Meliadus.

Baron Meliadus turned and motioned for the guards to leave. Then he pulled a cord, and tapestries rippled down the walls to hide the mirrors. Hawkmoon could still look up or down and see his own reflection if he desired. Instead he looked out of the window.

A thick fog covered the city, swirling green-black about the towers, obscuring the river. It was evening, with the sun almost completely set, and the towers looked like strange, unnatural rock formations, jutting from a primordial sea. If a great reptile had risen from it and pressed an eye to the grimy moisture-streaked window it would not have been surprising.

Without the wall mirrors, the room became even gloomier, for there was no artificial source of light. The baron, framed against the window, hummed to himself, ignoring Hawkmoon.

From somewhere in the depths of the city a faint distorted cry echoed through the fog and then faded. Baron Meliadus lifted his wolf mask and looked carefully at Hawkmoon, whom he could now barely see. "Come nearer to the window, my lord," he said. Hawkmoon moved forward, his feet slipping once or twice on the rugs that partially covered the glass floor.

"Well," Meliadus began, "I have spoken to Baron Kalan, and he reports an enigma, a psyche he can hardly interpret. He said it seemed that some part of it had died. What did it die of? I wonder. Of grief? Of humiliation? Of fear? I had not expected such complications. I had expected to bargain with you man to man, trading something you desired for a service I required of you. While I see no reason not to continue to obtain this service, I am not altogether sure, now, how to go about it. Would you consider a bargain, my lord Duke?"

"What do you propose?" Hawkmoon stared beyond the baron, through the window at the darkening sky.

"You have heard of Count Brass, the old hero?"

"Yes."

"He is now Lord Guardian, Protector of the Province of Kamarg."

"I have heard that."

"He has proved stubborn in opposing the will of the King-Emperor, he has insulted Granbretan. We wish to encourage wisdom in him. The way to do this will be to capture his daughter, who is dear to him, and bring her to Granbretan as a hostage. However, he would trust no emissary that we sent nor any common stranger—but he must have heard of your exploits at the Battle of Köln and doubtless sympathizes with you. If you were to go to Kamarg seeking sanctuary from the Empire of Granbretan, he would almost certainly welcome you. Once within his walls, it would not be too difficult for a man of your resourcefulness to pick the right moment, abduct the girl, bring her back to us. Beyond the borders of Kamarg we should, naturally, be able to give you plenty of support. Kamarg is a small territory. You could easily escape."

"That is what you desire of me?"

"Just so. In return we give you back your estates to rule as you please so long as you take no part against the Dark Empire, whether in word or deed."

"My people live in misery under Granbretan," Hawkmoon said suddenly, as if in revelation. He spoke without passion but rather like one making an abstract moral decision. "It would be better for them if I ruled them."

"Ah!" Baron Meliadus smiled. "So my bargain does seem reasonable!"

"Yes, though I do not believe you will keep your part of it."

"Why not? It is essentially to our advantage if a troublesome state can be ruled by someone whom it trusts—and whom we may trust also."

"I will go to Kamarg. I will tell them the tale you suggest. I will capture the girl and bring her to Granbretan." Hawkmoon sighed and looked at Baron Meliadus. "Why not?"

Discomfited by the strangeness of Hawkmoon's manner, unused to dealing with such a personality, Meliadus frowned. "We cannot be absolutely sure that you are not indulging in some complex form of deceit to trick us into releasing you. Although the mentality machine is infallible in the case of all other subjects who have been tested by it, it could be that you are aware of some secret sorcery that confuses it."

"I know nothing of sorcery."

"So I believe—almost." Baron Meliadus's tone became somewhat cheerful. "But we have no need to fear—there is an excellent precaution we can take against any treachery from you. A precaution that will bring you back to us or kill you if we have reason no longer to trust you. It is a device recently discovered by Baron Kalan, though I understand it is not his original invention. It is called the Black Jewel. You will be supplied with it tomorrow. Tonight you will sleep in apartments prepared for you in the palace. Before you leave you will have the honour of being presented to His Majesty the King-Emperor. Few foreigners are granted so much."

With that, Meliadus called to the insect-masked guards and ordered them to escort Hawkmoon to his quarters.

3

THE BLACK JEWEL

Next morning, Dorian Hawkmoon was taken to see Baron Kalan again. The serpent mask seemed to bear an almost cynical expression as it regarded him, but the baron said hardly a word, merely led him through a series of rooms and halls until they reached a room with a door of plain steel. This was opened, to reveal a similar door that, when opened, revealed a third door. This led into a small, blindingly lighted chamber of white metal that contained a machine of intense beauty. It consisted almost entirely of delicate red, gold, and silver webs, strands of which brushed Hawkmoon's face and had the warmth and vitality of human skin. Faint music came from the webs, which moved as if in a breeze.

"It seems alive," said Hawkmoon.

"It is alive," Baron Kalan whispered proudly. "It is alive."

"Is it a beast?"

"No. It is the creation of sorcery. I am not even sure what it is. I built it according to the instructions of a grimoire I bought from an Easterner many years ago. It is the machine of the Black Jewel. Ah, and soon you will become much more intimately acquainted with it, lord Duke."

Deep within him, Hawkmoon felt a faint stirring of panic, but it did not begin to rise to the surface of his mind. He let the strands of red and gold and silver caress him.

"It is not complete," Kalan said. "It must spin the Jewel. Move closer to it, my lord. Move *in* to it. You will feel no pain, I guarantee. It must spin the Black Jewel."

Hawkmoon obeyed the baron, and the webs rustled and began to sing. His ears became confounded, the traceries of red, gold, and silver confused his eyes. The machine of the Black Jewel fondled him, seemed to enter him, become him and he it. He sighed, and his voice was the music of the webs; he moved and his limbs were tenuous strands.

There was pressure from within his skull, and he felt a sense of absolute warmth and softness suffuse his body. He drifted as if bodiless and lost the sense of passing time, but he knew that the machine was spinning something from its own substance, making something that became hard and dense and implanted itself in his forehead so that suddenly he seemed to possess a third eye and stared out at the world with a new kind of vision. Then gradually this faded and he was looking at Baron Kalan, who had removed his mask, the better to regard him.

Hawkmoon felt a sudden sharp pain in his head. The pain vanished almost at once. He looked back at the machine, but its colours had dulled and its webs seemed to have shrunk. He lifted a hand to his forehead and felt with a shock something there that had not been there before. It was hard and smooth. It was part of him. He shuddered.

Baron Kalan looked concerned. "Eh? You are not mad, are you? I was sure of success! You are not mad?"

"I am not mad," Hawkmoon said. "But I think that I am afraid."

"You will become accustomed to the Jewel."

"That is what is in my head? The Jewel?"

"Aye. The Black Jewel. Wait." Kalan turned and drew aside a curtain of scarlet velvet, revealing a flat oval of milky quartz about two feet long. In it, a picture began to form. Hawkmoon saw that the picture was that of Kalan staring into the quartz oval, into infinity. The screen revealed exactly what Hawkmoon saw. As he turned his head slightly, the picture altered accordingly.

Kalan muttered in delight. "It works, you see. What you perceive, the Jewel perceives. Wherever you go we shall be able to see everything and everyone you encounter."

Hawkmoon tried to speak, but he could not. His throat was tight, and there seemed to be something constricting his lungs. Again he touched the warm Jewel, so similar to flesh in texture, but so unlike it in every other way.

"What have you done to me?" he asked eventually, his tone as flat as ever.

"We have merely secured your loyalty," chuckled Kalan. "You have taken part of the life of the machine. Should we so desire, we can give all the machine's life to the Jewel, and then . . . ."

Hawkmoon reached out stiffly and touched the baron's arm. "What will it do?"

"It will eat your brain, Duke of Köln."

Baron Meliadus hurried Dorian Hawkmoon through the glittering passages of the palace. Now Hawkmoon had a sword at his side and a suit of clothes and mail much like those he had worn at the Battle of Köln. He was conscious of the jewel in his skull but of little else. The passages widened until they covered the area of a good-sized street. Guards in the masks of the Order of the Mantis were thick along the walls. Mighty doors, a mass of jewels making mosaic patterns, towered ahead of them.

"The throne room," murmured the baron. "Now the King-Emperor will inspect you."

Slowly the doors moved open, to reveal the glory of the throne room. It blazed, half-blinding Hawkmoon with its magnificence. There was glitter and music; from a dozen galleries that rose to the concave roof were draped the shimmering banners of five hundred of Granbretan's noblest families. Lining the walls and galleries, rigid with their flame-lances at the salute, were the soldiers of the Order of the Mantis in their insect-masks and their plate armour of black, green, and gold. Behind them, in a multitude of different masks and a profusion of rich clothing, were the courtiers. They peered curiously at Meliadus and Hawkmoon as they entered.

The lines of soldiers stretched into the distance. There, at the end of the hall, almost out of sight, hung something that Hawkmoon could not at first make out. He frowned. "The Throne Globe," whispered Meliadus. "Now do as I do." He began to pace forward.

The walls of the throne room were of lustrous green and purple, but the colours of the banners ranged the spectrum, as did the fabrics, metals, and precious gems that the courtiers wore. But Hawkmoon's eyes were fixed on the globe.

Dwarfed by the proportions of the throne room, Hawkmoon and Meliadus walked with measured pace toward the Throne Globe while fanfares were played by trumpeters in the galleries to left and right.

Eventually Hawkmoon could see the Throne Globe, and he was astonished. It contained a milky-white fluid that surged about sluggishly, almost hypnotically. At times the fluid seemed to contain iridescent radiance that would gradually fade and then return. In the centre of this fluid, reminding Hawkmoon of a foetus, drifted an ancient man, his skin wrinkled, his limbs apparently useless, his head overlarge. From this head stared sharp, malicious eyes.

Following Meliadus's example, Hawkmoon abased himself before the creature.

"Rise," came a voice. Hawkmoon realized with a shock that the voice came from the globe. It was the voice of a young man in the prime of health—a golden voice, a melodic, vibrant voice. Hawkmoon wondered from what youthful throat the voice had been torn.

"King-Emperor, I present Dorian Hawkmoon, Duke von Köln, who has elected to perform an errand for us. You'll remember, noble sire, that I mentioned my plan to you . . ." Meliadus bowed as he spoke.

"We go to much effort and considerable ingenuity to secure the services of this Count Brass," came the golden voice. "We trust your judgment is sound in this matter, Baron Meliadus."

"You have reason to trust me on the strength of my past deeds, Great Majesty," Meliadus said, again bowing.

"Has the Duke von Köln been warned of the inevitable penalty he will pay if he does not serve us loyally?" came the youthful, sardonic voice. "Has he been told that we may destroy him in an instant, from any distance?"

Meliadus stroked his sleeve. "He has, Mighty King-Emperor."

"You have informed him that the Jewel in his skull," continued the voice with relish, "sees all that he sees and shows it to us in the chamber of the machine of the Black Jewel?"

"Aye, Noble Monarch."

"And you have made it clear to him that should he show any signs of betraying us—any slight sign, which we may easily detect by watching through his eyes the faces of those he speaks to—we shall give the Jewel its full life? We shall release all the energy of the machine into its sibling. Have you told him, Baron Meliadus, that the Jewel, possessed of its full life, will then eat its way through his brain, devour his mind, and turn him into a drooling, mindless creature?"

"In essence, Great Emperor, he has been so informed."

The thing in the Throne Globe chuckled. "By the look of him, Baron, the threat of mindlessness is no threat at all. Are you sure he's not already possessed of the Jewel's full life?"

"It is his character to seem thus, Immortal Ruler."

Now the eyes turned to peer into those of Dorian Hawkmoon, and the sardonic, golden voice issued from the infinitely aged throat.

"You have contracted a bargain, Duke von Köln, with the immortal King-Emperor of Granbretan. It is a testament to our liberality that we should offer such a bargain to one who is, after all, our slave. You must serve us, in turn, with great loyalty, knowing that you share a part in the destiny of the greatest race ever to emerge on this planet. It is our right to rule the Earth, by virtue of our omniscient intellect and omnipotent might, and soon we shall claim this right in full. All who help serve our noble purpose will receive our approval. Go now, Duke, and win that approval."

The wizened head turned, and a prehensile tongue flickered from the mouth to touch a tiny jewel that drifted near the wall of the Throne Globe. The globe began to dim until the foetuslike shape of the King-Emperor, last and immortal descendant of a dynasty founded almost three thousand years before, appeared for a few moments in silhouette. "And remember the power of the Black Jewel," said the youthful voice before the globe took on the appearance of a solid, dull black sphere.

The audience was ended. Abasing themselves, Meliadus and Hawkmoon backed away a few paces and then turned to walk from the throne room. And the audience had served a purpose not anticipated by the baron or his master. Within Hawkmoon's strange mind, in its most hidden depths, a tiny irritation had begun; and the irritation was caused not by the Black Jewel that lay embedded in his forehead, but by a less tangible source.

Perhaps the irritation was a sign of Hawkmoon's humanity returning. Perhaps it marked the growing of a new and altogether different quality; perhaps it was the influence of the Runestaff.

4

JOURNEY TO CASTLE BRASS

Dorian Hawkmoon was returned to his original apartments in the prison catacombs and there waited for two days until Baron Meliadus arrived, bearing with him a suit of black leather, complete with boots and gauntlets, a heavy black cloak with a cowl, a silver-hilted broadsword in a black leather scabbard, simply decorated with silver, and a black helmet-mask wrought in the likeness of a snarling wolf. The clothes and equipment were evidently modeled on Meliadus's own.

"Your tale, on reaching Castle Brass," Meliadus began, "will be a fine one. You were made prisoner by myself and managed, with the aid of a slave, to drug me and pose as me. In this disguise you crossed Granbretan and all the provinces she controls before Meliadus recovered from the drug. A simple story is the best, and this one serves not only to answer how you came to escape from

Granbretan, but also to elevate you in the eyes of those who hate me."

"I understand," Hawkmoon said, fingering the heavy black jacket. "But how is the Black Jewel explained?"

"You were to be the subject of some experiment of mine but escaped before any serious harm could be done to you. Tell the story well, Hawkmoon, for your safety will depend on it. We shall be watching the reaction of Count Brass—and particularly that wily rhyme maker Bowgentle. Though we shall be unable to hear what you say, we can read lips well enough. Any sign of betrayal on your part—and we give the Jewel its full life."

"I understand," Hawkmoon repeated in the same flat tone.

Meliadus frowned. "They will evidently note your strangeness of manner, but with luck they will explain it by the misfortunes you have suffered. It could make them even more solicitous."

Hawkmoon nodded vaguely.

Meliadus looked at him sharply. "I am still troubled by you, Hawkmoon. I am still unsure that you have not by some sorcery or cunning deceived us—but nonetheless I am certain of your loyalty. The Black Jewel is my assurance." He smiled. "Now, an ornithopter is waiting to take you to Deau-Vere and the coast. Ready yourself, my lord Duke, and serve Granbretan faithfully. If you are successful, you shall soon be master of your own estates again."

The ornithopter had settled on the lawns beyond the city entrance to the catacombs. It was a thing of great beauty, fashioned in the shape of a gigantic griffin, all worked in copper, brass, silver, and black steel, squatting on its powerful lionlike haunches, the forty-foot wings folded on its back. Below the head, in the small cockpit, sat the pilot, dressed in the bird-mask of his Order— the Order of the Crow, which was comprised of all flyers—his gloved hands on the jeweled controls.

With some wariness, Hawkmoon, now clad in the costume that so resembled Meliadus's, climbed in behind the pilot, finding difficulty with his sword as he tried to seat himself in the long, narrow seat. Eventually he settled into a position of comparative comfort and gripped the ribbed metal sides of the flying machine as the pilot depressed a lever and the wings clashed open and began to beat the air with a strange, echoing boom. The whole ornithopter shuddered and listed to one side for an instant before the pilot, cursing, had it under control. Hawkmoon had heard that there were dangers in flying these machines and had seen several that had attacked him at Köln suddenly fold their wings behind them and hurtle to the ground. But in spite of their instabilities, the ornithopters of the Dark Empire had been the chief weapon in conquering so speedily the mainland of Europe, for no other race possessed flying machines of any kind.

Now, with an uncomfortable jerking motion, the metal griffin slowly began to ascend. The wings thrashed the air, a parody of natural flight, and they climbed higher and higher until they had cleared the tops of Londra's tallest towers and were circling toward the south-east. Hawkmoon breathed heavily, disliking the unfamiliar sensation.

Soon the monster had passed above a heavy layer of dark cloud, and sunshine flashed on its metal scales. His face and eyes protected by the mask, through whose jeweled eyes he peered,

Hawkmoon saw the sunlight refracted into a million rainbow flashes. He closed his eyes.

Time passed, and he felt the ornithopter begin to descend. He opened his eyes and saw that they were deep within the clouds again, breaking through them to see ash-grey fields, the outline of a turreted city, and the livid, rolling sea beyond.

Clumsily, the machine flapped toward a great, flat stretch of rock that rose from the centre of the city.

It landed with a heavy bumping motion, wings beating frenetically, and at last halted close to the edge of the artificial plateau.

The pilot signaled for Hawkmoon to get out. He did so, feeling stiff, his legs shaking, while the pilot locked his controls and joined him on the ground. Here and there were other ornithopters. As they walked across the rock beneath the lowering sky, one began to flap into the air, and Hawkmoon felt wind slap against his face from the wings as the thing passed close above his head.

"Deau-Vere," the crow-masked pilot said. "A port given over almost wholly to our aerial navies, although ships of war still use the harbour."

Soon Hawkmoon could see a circular steel hatch in the rock ahead of them. The pilot paused beside it and tapped out a complicated series of beats with his booted foot. Eventually the hatch swung downward, revealing a stone stairway, and they descended, while the hatch swung shut above them. The interior was gloomy, with decorations of glowering stone gargoyles and some inferior bas-reliefs.

At last they emerged through a guarded door into a paved street between the square, turreted buildings that filled the city. The streets were crowded with the warriors of Granbretan. Groups

of crow-masked flyers rubbed shoulders with the fish- and sea-
serpent-masked crews of the men-o'-war, the infantrymen and
the cavalry in a great variety of masks, some of the Order of the
Pig, others of the Orders of Wolf, Skull, Mantis, Bull, Hound,
Goat, and many more. Swords slapped armoured legs, flame-lances
clashed in the press, and everywhere was the gloomy jingle of
military gear.

Pushing through this throng, Hawkmoon was surprised that it
gave way so easily, until he remembered how closely he must resemble Baron Meliadus.

At the gates of the city there was a horse waiting for him, its
saddle panniers bulging with provisions. Hawkmoon had already
been told about the horse and which road he must follow. He
mounted the animal and cantered toward the sea.

Very soon the clouds parted and sunshine broke through them,
and Dorian Hawkmoon saw for the first time the Silver Bridge that
spanned thirty miles of sea. It flashed in the sunlight, a beautiful
thing, seemingly too delicate to withstand the merest breeze but
actually strong enough to bear all the armies of Granbretan. It
curved away over the ocean, beyond the horizon. The causeway
itself measured almost a quarter of a mile across, flanked by quiv-
ering networks of silver hawsers supported by pylon archways,
intricately moulded in military motifs.

Across this bridge passed to and fro a splendid variety of traffic.
Hawkmoon could see carriages of nobles, so elaborate that it was
hard to believe they could function; squadrons of cavalry, the horses
as magnificently armoured as their riders; battalions of infantry,
marching four abreast with unbelievable precision; trading caravans of carts; and beasts of burden with swaying stacks of every

conceivable kind of goods—furs, silks, meat carcasses, fruit, vegetables, chests of treasure, candlesticks, beds, whole suites of chairs—much of which, Hawkmoon realized, was loot from states like Köln recently conquered by those same armies who passed the caravans.

War engines, too, he could see—things of iron and copper— with cruel beaks for ramming, high towers for the siege, long beams for hurling massive fireballs and boulders. Marching beside them, in masks of mole and badger and ferret, were the engineers of the Dark Empire, with squat, powerful bodies and large, heavy hands. All these things took on the aspect of ants, dwarfed as they were by the majesty of the Silver Bridge, which, like the ornithopters, had contributed greatly to the ease of Granbretan's conquests.

The guards on the bridge's gateway had been told to let Hawkmoon pass, and the gateway opened as he neared it. He rode straight onto the vibrating bridge, his horse's hoofs clattering on the metal. The causeway, seen at this range, lost some of its magnificence. Its surface had been scored and dented by the passage of the traffic. Here and there were piles of horse dung, rags, straw, and less recognizable refuse. It was impossible to keep such a well-used thoroughfare in perfect condition, but somehow the soiled causeway symbolized something of the spirit of the strange civilization of Granbretan.

Hawkmoon crossed the Silver Bridge across the sea and came, after some time, to the mainland of Europe, making his way toward the Crystal City so lately conquered by the Dark Empire; the Crystal City of Parye, where he would rest for a day before beginning his journey south.

But he had more than a day's journey before he came to the Crystal City, no matter how hard he rode. He decided not to stay in Karlye, the city closest to the bridge, but to find a village where he might rest for that night and then continue in the morning.

Just before sunset he reached a village of pleasant villas and gardens that bore the marks of conflict. Indeed, some of the villas were in ruins. The village was strangely quiet, though a few lights were beginning to burn in windows, and the inn, when he reached it, had its doors closed and there were no signs of revelry from within. He dismounted in the inn's courtyard and banged on the door with his fist. He waited for several minutes before the bar was withdrawn and a boy's face peered out at him. The boy looked frightened when he saw the wolf mask. Reluctantly he drew the door open to let Hawkmoon enter. As soon as he was inside, Hawkmoon pushed back the mask and tried to smile at the boy to give him reassurance, but the smile was artificial, for Hawkmoon had forgotten how to move his lips correctly. The boy seemed to take the expression as one of disapproval, and he backed away, his eyes half-defiant, as if expecting a blow at the very least.

"I mean you no harm," Hawkmoon said stiffly. "Only take care of my horse and give me a bed and some food. I'll leave at dawn."

"Master, we have only the humblest food," murmured the boy, partly reassured. The people of Europe in these days were used to occupation by this faction or that, and the conquest of Granbretan was not, in essence, a new experience. The ferocity of the people of the Dark Empire was new, however, and this was plainly what the boy feared and hated, expecting not even the roughest justice from one who was evidently a noble of Granbretan.

"I'll take whatever you have. Save your best food and wine if you will. I seek only to satisfy my hunger and sleep."

"Sire, our best food is all gone. If we—"

Hawkmoon silenced him with a gesture. "I am not interested, boy. Take me literally and you will serve me best."

He looked about the room and noted one or two old men sitting in the shadows, drinking from heavy tankards and avoiding looking at him. He went to the centre of the room and seated himself at a small table, stripping off his cloak and gauntlets and wiping the dust of the road from his face and body. The wolf mask he dumped on the ground beside his chair, a most uncharacteristic gesture for a noble of the Dark Empire. He noticed one of the men glance at him in some surprise, and when a murmur broke out a little later, he realized they had seen the Black Jewel. The boy returned with thin ale and some scraps of pork, and Hawkmoon had the feeling that this was, indeed, their best. He ate the pork and drank the ale and then called to be taken to his room. Once in the sparsely furnished chamber he stripped off his gear, bathed himself, climbed between the rough sheets, and was soon asleep.

During the night he was disturbed, without realizing what had awakened him. For some reason he felt drawn to the window and looked out. In the moonlight he thought he saw a figure on a heavy warhorse, looking up at his window. The figure was that of a warrior in full armour, his visor covering his face. Hawkmoon believed he caught a flash of jet and gold. Then the warrior had turned his horse and disappeared.

Feeling that there was some significance to this event, Hawkmoon returned to his bed. He slept again, quite as soundly as before, but in the morning he was not sure whether he had dreamed or not. If it had been a dream, then it was the first he had had since he had been captured. A twinge of curiosity made him frown slightly as he dressed himself, but he shrugged then and went down to the main room of the inn to ask for some breakfast.

Hawkmoon reached the Crystal City by the evening. Its buildings of purest quartz were alive with colour, and everywhere was the tinkle of the glass decorations that the citizens of Parye used to adorn their houses and public buildings and monuments. Such a beautiful city it was that even the warlords of the Dark Empire had left it almost wholly intact, preferring to take the city by stealth and waste several months, rather than attack it.

But within the city the marks of occupation were everywhere, from the look of permanent fear on the faces of the common folk, to the beast-masked warriors who swaggered the streets, and the flags that flowed in the wind over the houses once owned by Parye's noblemen. Now the flags were those of Jerek Nankenseen, Warlord of the Order of the Fly; Adaz Promp, Grand Constable of the Order of the Hound; Mygel Holst, Archduke of Londra; and Asrovak Mikosevaar, renegade of Muskovia, mercenary Warlord of the Vulture Legion, pervert and destroyer, whose legion had served Granbretan even before her plan of European conquest became evident. A madman to match even those insane nobles of Granbretan he allowed to be his masters, Asrovak Mikosevaar was always at the forefront of Granbretan's armies, pushing the boundaries of Empire onward. His infamous banner, with the words stitched in scarlet on it, *Death to Life!* struck fear into the hearts of all who fought against it. Asrovak Mikosevaar must be resting in the Crystal City, Hawkmoon decided, for it was unlike him to be far from any battle line. Corpses drew the Muskovian as roses drew bees.

There were no children in the streets of the Crystal City. Those who had not been slaughtered by Granbretan had been imprisoned by the conquerors, to ensure the good behaviour of the citizens who remained alive.

The sun seemed to stain the crystal buildings with blood as it set, and Hawkmoon, too weary to ride on, was forced to find the inn Meliadus had told him of and there sleep for the best part of a night and a day before resuming his journey to Castle Brass. There was still more than half of that journey to finish.

Beyond the city of Lyon, the Empire of Granbretan had so far been checked in its conquests, but the road to Lyon was a bleak road, lined with gibbets and wooden crosses on which hung men and women, young and old, girls and boys, and even, perhaps as an insane jest, domestic pets such as cats, dogs, and tame rabbits. Whole families rotted there; entire households, from the youngest baby to the oldest servant, were nailed in attitudes of agony to the crosses.

The stench of decay inflamed Hawkmoon's nostrils as he let his horse plod miserably down the Lyon Road, and the stink of death clogged his throat. Fire had blackened fields and forests, razed towns and villages, turned the very air grey and heavy. All who lived had become beggars, whatever their former station, save those women who had become whores to the Empire's soldiery, or those men who had sworn groveling allegiance to the King-Emperor.

As curiosity had touched him earlier, now disgust stirred faintly in Hawkmoon's breast, but he hardly noticed it. Wolf-masked, he rode on toward Lyon. None stopped him; none questioned him, for those who served the Order of the Wolf were, in the main, fighting in the north, and thus Hawkmoon was safe from any Wolf addressing him in the secret language of the Order.

Beyond Lyon, Hawkmoon took to the fields, for the roads were patrolled by Granbretanian warriors. He stuffed his wolf-mask into one of his now empty panniers and rode swiftly into the free territory where the air was still sweet but where terror still blossomed, save that this was a terror of the future rather than of the present.

In the town of Valence, where warriors prepared to meet the attack of the Dark Empire when it came—discussing hopeless stratagems, building inadequate war engines—Hawkmoon told his story first.

"I am Dorian Hawkmoon von Köln," he told the captain to whom the soldiers took him.

The captain, one thigh-booted foot on a bench in the crowded inn, stared at him carefully. "The Duke von Köln must be dead by now—he was captured by Granbretan," he said. "I think you are a spy."

Hawkmoon did not protest but told the story Meliadus had given him. Speaking expressionlessly, he described his capture and his method of escape, and his strange tone convinced the captain more than the story itself. Then a swordsman in battered mail pushed through the crowd shouting Hawkmoon's name.

Turning, Hawkmoon recognized the insignia on the man's coat as his own, the arms of Köln. The man was one of the few who had fled the Köln battlefield somehow. He spoke to the captain and the crowd, describing the duke's bravery and ingenuity. Then Dorian Hawkmoon was heralded as a hero in Valence.

That night, while his coming was celebrated, Hawkmoon told the captain that he was bound for Kamarg to try to recruit the help of Count Brass in the war against Granbretan. The captain shook his head. "Count Brass takes no sides," he said. "But it is likely he will listen to you rather than anyone else. I hope you are successful, my lord Duke."

Next morning, Hawkmoon rode away from Valence, rode down the trail to the south, while grim-faced men passed him riding north to join forces with those preparing to withstand the Dark Empire.

The wind blew harder and harder as Hawkmoon neared his destination and saw, at length, the flat marshlands of Kamarg, the lagoons shining in the distance, the reeds bent beneath the mistral's force—a lonely, lovely land. When he passed close to one of the tall old towers and saw the heliograph begin to flash, he knew that his coming would be newsed to Castle Brass before he arrived there.

Cold-faced, Hawkmoon sat his horse stiffly as it picked its way along the winding marsh road where shrubs swayed and water rippled and a few birds floated through the sad old skies.

Shortly before nightfall, Castle Brass came in sight, its terraced hill and delicate towers a black-and-grey silhouette against the evening.

5

THE AWAKENING OF HAWKMOON

Count Brass passed Dorian Hawkmoon a fresh cup of wine and murmured, "Please continue, my lord Duke," as Hawkmoon told his story for the second time. In the hall of Castle Brass sat Yisselda, in all her beauty, Bowgentle, thoughtful of countenance, and von Villach, who stroked his moustache and stared at the fire.

Hawkmoon finished the tale. "And so I sought help in Kamarg, Count Brass, knowing that only this land is secure from the power of the Dark Empire."

"You are welcome here," Count Brass said, frowning. "If refuge is all you seek."

"That is all."

"You do not come to ask us to take arms against Granbretan?" It was Bowgentle who spoke, half-hopefully.

"I have suffered enough from doing so myself—for the time being—and would not wish to encourage others to risk meeting a fate I only narrowly missed myself," replied Hawkmoon.

Yisselda looked almost disappointed. It was plain that all in the room, save wise Count Brass, wanted war with Granbretan. For different reasons, perhaps—Yisselda to revenge herself against Meliadus, Bowgentle because he believed such evil must be countered, von Villach simply because he wished to exercise his sword again.

"Good," said Count Brass, "for I'm tired of resisting arguments that I should help this faction or that. Now—you seem exhausted, my lord Duke. Indeed, I have rarely seen a man so tired. We have kept you up too long. I will personally show you to your chambers."

Hawkmoon felt no triumph in having accomplished his deception. He told the lies because he had agreed with Meliadus that he would tell such lies. When the time came for kidnapping Yisselda, he would pursue the task in the same spirit.

Count Brass showed him into a suite consisting of bedchamber, washing room, and a small study. "I hope it is to your taste, my lord Duke?"

"Completely," Hawkmoon replied.

Count Brass paused by the door. "The Jewel," he said, "the one in your forehead—you say that Meliadus was unsuccessful in his experiment?"

"That is so, Count."

"Aha . . ." Count Brass looked at the floor, then, after a moment, glanced up again. "For I might know some sorcery that could remove it, if it troubles you . . ."

"It does not trouble me," said Hawkmoon.

"Aha," said the count again, and left the room.

That night, Hawkmoon awoke suddenly, as he had awakened in the inn a few nights since, and thought he saw a figure in the room—an armoured man in jet and gold. His heavy lids fell shut for a moment or two, and when he opened them again the figure was gone.

A conflict was beginning to develop in Hawkmoon's breast—perhaps a conflict between humanity and the lack of it, perhaps a conflict between conscience and the lack of conscience, if such conflicts were possible.

Whatever the exact nature of the conflict, there was no doubt that Hawkmoon's character was changing for a second time. It was not the character he had had on the battlefield at Köln, nor the strange apathetic mood into which he had fallen since the battle, but a new character altogether, as if Hawkmoon were being born again in a thoroughly different mould.

But the indications of this birth were still faint, and a catalyst was needed, as well as a climate in which the birth would be possible.

Meanwhile, Hawkmoon woke up in the morning thinking how he might most speedily accomplish the capture of Yisselda and return to Granbretan to be rid of the Black Jewel and sent back to the land of his youth.

Bowgentle met him as he left his chambers.

The philosopher-poet took his arm. "Ah, my lord Duke, perhaps you could tell me something of Londra. I was never there, though I traveled a great deal when I was younger."

Hawkmoon turned to look at Bowgentle, knowing that the face he saw would be the same as the nobles of Granbretan would see by means of the Black Jewel. There was an expression of frank interest in Bowgentle's eyes, and Hawkmoon decided that the man did not suspect him.

"It is vast and high and dark," Hawkmoon replied. "The architecture is involved, and the decoration complex and various."

"And its spirit? What is the spirit of Londra—what was your impression?"

"Power," said Hawkmoon. "Confidence . . ."

"Insanity?"

"I am incapable of knowing what is sane and what is not, Sir Bowgentle. You find me a strange man, perhaps? My manner is awkward? My attitudes unlike those of other men?"

Surprised by this turn of the conversation, Bowgentle looked carefully at Hawkmoon. "Why, yes . . . but what is your reason for asking?"

"Because I find your questions all but meaningless. I say that without—without wishing to insult . . ." Hawkmoon rubbed his chin. "I find them meaningless, you see."

They began to descend the steps toward the main hall, where breakfast had been laid and where old von Villach was already serving himself a large steak from a salver held by a servant.

"Meaning," murmured Bowgentle. "You wonder what insanity is—I wonder what meaning is."

"I do not know," Hawkmoon answered. "I only know what I do."

"Your ordeal has driven you into yourself—abolished morality and conscience?" Bowgentle said with sympathy. "It is not an unfamiliar circumstance. Reading ancient texts, one learns of many who under duress lost the same senses. Good food and affectionate company should restore them to you. It was lucky you should come to Castle Brass. Perhaps an inner voice sent you to us."

Hawkmoon listened without interest, watching Yisselda descend the opposite staircase and smile at himself and Bowgentle across the hall.

"Are you well rested, my lord Duke?" she asked.

Before Hawkmoon could reply, Bowgentle said, "He has suffered more than we guessed. It will take our guest a week or two, I should think, before he is fully recovered."

"Perhaps you would like to accompany me this morning, my lord?" Yisselda suggested graciously. "I will show you our gardens. Even in winter they are beautiful."

"Yes," replied Hawkmoon, "I should like to see them."

Bowgentle smiled, realizing that Yisselda's warm heart had been touched by Hawkmoon's plight. There could be no-one better, he thought, than the girl to restore the duke's injured spirit.

They walked through the terraces of the castle gardens. Here were evergreens, there winter-blooming flowers and vegetables. The sky was clear and the sun shone down, and they did not suffer much discomfort from the wind, muffled as they were in heavy cloaks. They looked down on the roofs of the town, and all was at peace. Yisselda's arm was linked in Hawkmoon's, and she conversed lightly, expecting no reply from the sad-faced man at her side. The Black Jewel in his forehead had disturbed her a little at first, until she had decided that it was scarcely different from a jeweled circlet such as she sometimes wore to keep her long hair from her eyes.

She had much warmth and affection in her young heart. It was this affection that had turned to passion for Baron Meliadus, for it needed as many outlets as it could have. She was content to offer it to this strange, stiff hero of Köln and hope that it might heal the wounds of his spirit.

She soon noticed that a hint of expression only came into his eyes when she mentioned his homeland.

"Tell me of Köln," she said. "Not as it is now, but at it was—as one day it might be again."

Her words reminded Hawkmoon of Meliadus's promise to restore his lands. He looked away from the girl and up at the wind-blown sky, folding his arms across his chest.

"Köln," she said softly. "Was it like Kamarg?"

"No . . ." He turned to stare down at the rooftops far below. "No . . . for Kamarg is wild and as it has always been since the beginning of time. Köln bore the mark of Man everywhere—in its hedged fields and its straight watercourses—its little winding roads and its farms and villages. It was only a small province, with fat cows and well-fed sheep, with hayricks and meadows of soft grass that sheltered rabbits and fieldmice. It had yellow fences and cool woods, and the smoke from a chimney was never far from sight. Its people were simple and friendly and kind to small children. Its buildings were old and quaint and as simple as the people who lived in them. There was nothing dark in Köln till Granbretan came, a flood of harsh metal and fierce fire from across the Rhine. And Granbretan also put the mark of Man upon the countryside . . . the mark of the sword and the torch . . ."

He sighed, an increasing trace of emotion entering his tone. "The mark of the sword and the torch, replacing the mark of the plough and the harrow . . ." He turned to look at her. "And the cross and gibbet were made from the timber of the yellow fences, and the carcasses of the cows and sheep clogged the watercourses and poisoned the land, and the stones of the farmhouses became ammunition for the catapults, and the people became corpses or soldiers—there was no other choice."

She put her soft hand on his leathern arm. "You speak as if the memory were very distant," she said.

The expression faded from his eyes, and they became cold again. "So it is, so it is—like an old dream. It means little to me now."

But Yisselda looked at him thoughtfully as she led him through the gardens, thinking that she had found a way to reach him and help him.

For his part, Hawkmoon had been reminded of what he would lose if he did not carry the girl to the Dark Lords, and he welcomed her attention for reasons other than she guessed.

Count Brass met them in the courtyard. He was inspecting a large old warhorse and talking to a groom. "Put him out to graze," Count Brass said. "His service is over." Then he came toward Hawkmoon and his daughter. "Sir Bowgentle tells me you are wearier than we thought," he said to Hawkmoon. "But you are welcome to stay at Castle Brass for as long as you like. I hope Yisselda is not tiring you with her conversation."

"No. I find it . . . restful . . ."

"Good! Tonight we have an entertainment. I have asked Bowgentle to read to us from his latest work. He's promised to give us something light and witty. I hope you will enjoy it."

Hawkmoon noticed that Count Brass's eyes looked at him acutely, though his manner was hearty enough. Could Count Brass suspect his mission? The count was renowned for his wisdom and judgment of character. But surely if his character had baffled Baron Kalan, then it must also confuse the count. Hawkmoon decided that there was nothing to fear. He allowed Yisselda to lead him into the castle.

That night there was a banquet, with all Castle Brass's best laid out on the large board. Around the table sat several leading citizens of Kamarg, several bull breeders of repute, and several bullfighters, including the now-recovered Mahtan Just, whose life Count Brass had saved a year before. Fish and fowl, red meat and white, vegetables of every kind, wine of a dozen varieties, ale, and many delicious sauces and garnishes were heaped upon the long table. On Count Brass's right sat Dorian Hawkmoon, and on his left sat Mahtan Just, who had become that season's champion. Just plainly adored the count and treated him with a respect that the count seemed to find a trifle uncomfortable. Beside Hawkmoon sat Yisselda, and opposite her, Bowgentle. At the other end of the table was seated old Zhonzhac Ekare, greatest of the famous bull breeders, clad in heavy furs and with his face hidden by his huge beard and thick head of hair, laughing often and eating mightily. Beside him sat von Villach, and the two men seemed to enjoy each other's company a great deal.

When the feast was almost complete and pastries and sweetmeats and rich Kamarg cheese had been cleared, each guest had placed before him three flagons of wine of different kinds, a short barrel of ale, and a great drinking cup. Yisselda, alone, was given a single bottle and a smaller cup, though she had matched the men for drinking earlier and it seemed to be her choice, rather than the form, to drink less.

The wine had clouded Hawkmoon's mind a little and given him what was perhaps a spurious appearance of normal humanity. He smiled once or twice, and if he did not answer his companions jest for jest, at least he did not offend them with a sour expression.

Bowgentle's name was roared by Count Brass. "Bowgentle! The ballad you promised us!"

Bowgentle rose smiling, his face flushed, like the others', with the wine and the good food.

"I call this ballad 'The Emperor Glaucoma' and hope it will amuse you," he said, and began to speak the words.

> *The Emperor Glaucoma*
> *passed the formal*
> *guardsmen at the far arcade*
> *and entered the bazaar*
> *where the ornamental*
> *remnants of the last war,*
> *Knights Templar*
> *and the Ottoman,*
> *hosts of Alcazar*
> *and mighty Khan,*
> *lay in the shade*
> *of temple palms*

and called for alms.
But the Emperor Glaucoma
passed the lazar
undismayed
while pipes and tabor
played
in honour
of the Emperor's parade.

Count Brass was looking carefully at Bowgentle's grave face, a wry smile on his own lips. Meanwhile the poet spoke with wit and many graceful flourishes the complex rhyme. Hawkmoon looked about the board and saw some smiling, some looking puzzled, fuddled as they were by the drink. Hawkmoon neither smiled nor frowned. Yisselda bent toward him and murmured something, but he did not hear it.

The regatta
in the harbour
set off a cannonade
when the Emperor
displayed
stigmata
to the Vatican Ambassador

"What does he speak of?" grumbled von Villach.

"Ancient things," nodded old Zhonzhac Ekare, "before the Tragic Millennium."

"I'd rather hear a battle song."

Zhonzhac Ekare put a finger to his bearded lips and silenced his friend while Bowgentle continued.

> *who made*
> *gifts of alabaster,*
> *Damascus-blade,*
> *and Paris plaster*
> *from the tomb*
> *of Zoroaster*
> *where the nightshade*
> *and the oleaster*
> *bloom.*

Hawkmoon hardly heard the words, but the rhythms seemed to have a peculiar effect on him. At first he thought it was the wine, but then he realized that at certain points in the recitation his mind would seem to shudder and forgotten sensations would well up in his breast. He swayed in his chair.

Bowgentle looked hard at Hawkmoon as he continued his poem, gesticulating in an exaggerated way.

> *The poet laureate in laurel*
> *and orange brocade*
> *chased with topaz*
> *and opal*
> *and lucent jade,*
> *fragrant of pomander,*
> *redolent to myrrh*
> *and lavender,*

> *the treasure*
> *of Samarcand and Thrace,*
> *fell prostrate*
> *in the marketplace,*

"Are you well, my lord?" asked Yisselda, leaning toward Hawkmoon and speaking with concern.

Hawkmoon shook his head. "I am well enough, thanks." He was wondering if in some way he had offended the Lords of Granbretan and they were even now giving the Black Jewel its full life. His head was swimming.

> *insensate,*
> *and while choral*
> *anthems told*
> *his glory,*
> *the Emperor,*
> *majestical,*
> *in slippers of gold*
> *and ivory,*
> *upon him trod*
> *and throngs applaud*
> *the mortal god.*

Now all Hawkmoon saw was the figure and face of Bowgentle, heard nothing but the rhythms and the vowel rhymes, and wondered about enchantment. And if Bowgentle were seeking to enchant him, what was his reason?

From windows and towers
gaily arrayed
with garlands of flowers
and fresh bouquets
the children sprayed
showers
of meadow-rue,
roses and nosegays
of hyacinth into
the crossways
where Glaucoma passed.
Down to the causeways
from steeples and parapets
children threw
violets,
plum blossoms, lilies
and peonies,
and, last,
themselves
when Glaucoma passed.

Hawkmoon took a long draft of wine and breathed deeply, staring at Bowgentle as the poet continued with his verse.

The moon
shone dim,
the hot sun swayed
and still delayed

the noon,
the stars bestrewn
with seraphim
upraised
a hymn,
for soon
the Emperor
would stand before the sacred ruin
sublime
and lay his hand upon that door
unknown to time
that he alone
of mortal man may countermand.

Hawkmoon gasped as a man might when plunged into icy water. Yisselda's hand was on his sweat-wet brow, and her sweet eyes were troubled. "My lord . . . ?"

Hawkmoon stared at Bowgentle as the poet went relentlessly on.

Glaucoma passed
with eyes downcast
the grave ancestral portal
inlaid with precious stone
and pearl and bone
and ruby. He passed
the portal and the colonnade while trombone
sounds and trumpets blast
and earth trembles
and above

a host assembles
and the scent of ambergris is
burning in the air.

Dimly, Hawkmoon glimpsed Yisselda's hand touching his face, but he did not hear what she said. His eyes were fixed on Bowgentle, his ears were concentrated on listening to the verse. A goblet had fallen from his hand. He was plainly ill, but Count Brass made no move to help. Count Brass, instead, looked from Hawkmoon to Bowgentle, his face half-hidden behind his wine cup, an ironic expression in his eyes.

Now the Emperor releases
a snow-white dove!
O, a dove
as fair
as peace is,
so rare
that love increases
everywhere.

Hawkmoon groaned. At the far end of the table von Villach banged his wine cup on the table. "I'd agree with that. Why not 'The Mountain Bloodletting'? It's a good . . ."

The Emperor released
that snow-white dove
and it flew
till none could sight

it, flew through the bright
air, flew through fire,
flew still higher,
still flew higher,
right
into the sun
to die for
the Emperor Glaucoma

Hawkmoon staggered to his feet, tried to speak to Bowgentle, fell across the table, spilling wine in all directions.

"Is he drunk?" von Villach asked in a tone of disgust.

"He is ill!" called Yisselda. "Oh, he is ill!"

"He is not drunk, I think," Count Brass said, leaning over Hawkmoon's body and raising an eyelid. "But he is certainly insensible." He looked up at Bowgentle and smiled. Bowgentle smiled back and then shrugged.

"I hope you are sure of that, Count Brass," he said.

Hawkmoon lay all night in a deep coma and awoke the next morning to find Bowgentle, who acted as physician to the castle, bending over him. Whether what had happened had been caused by drink, the Black Jewel, or Bowgentle, he still could not be sure. Now he felt hot and weak.

"A fever, my lord Duke," Bowgentle said softly. "But we shall cure you, never fear."

Then Yisselda was there, seating herself beside his bed. She smiled at him. "Bowgentle says it is not serious," she told him. "I will nurse you. Soon you will be in good health again."

Hawkmoon looked into her face and felt a great flood of emotion fill him. "Lady Yisselda . . ."

"Yes, my lord?"

"I . . . thank you . . ."

He looked about the room in bewilderment. From behind him he heard a voice speak urgently. It was Count Brass's voice. "Say nothing more. Rest. Control your thoughts. Sleep if you can."

Hawkmoon had not realized Count Brass was in the room. Now Yisselda put a glass to his lips. He drank the cool liquid and was soon asleep again.

The next day the fever was gone, and rather than an absence of emotion, Dorian Hawkmoon felt as if he were numbed physically and spiritually. He wondered if he had been drugged.

Yisselda came to him as he was finishing breakfast and asked if he were ready to accompany her on a walk through the gardens, since the day was fine for the season.

He rubbed his head, feeling the strange warmth of the Black Jewel beneath his hand. With some alarm, he dropped his hand.

"Do you still feel ill, my lord?" asked Yisselda.

"No . . . I . . ." Hawkmoon sighed. "I don't know. I feel odd—it's unfamiliar . . ."

"Some fresh air, perhaps, will clear your head."

Passively, Hawkmoon got up to go with her into the gardens. The gardens were scented with all kinds of pleasant smells, and the sun was bright, making the shrubs and trees stand out sharply in the clear winter air.

The touch of Yisselda's arm linked in his stirred Hawkmoon's feelings further. It was a pleasant sensation, as was the bite of the wind in his face and the sight of the terraced gardens and the houses below. As well as these, he felt fear and distrust—fear of the Black Jewel, for he was sure that it would destroy him if he betrayed any sign of what he was now going through; and distrust of Count Brass and the rest, for he felt that they were in some way deceiving him and had more than an inkling of his purpose in coming to Castle Brass. He could seize the girl now, steal a horse, and perhaps stand a good chance of escaping. He looked at her suddenly.

Sweetly, she smiled up at him. "Has the air made you feel better, my lord Duke?"

He stared down into her face while many emotions conflicted within him. "Better?" he said hoarsely. "Better? I am not sure . . ."

"Are you tired?"

"No." His head had begun to ache, and again he felt afraid of the Black Jewel. He reached out and grasped the girl.

Thinking that he was falling from weakness, she took his arms and tried to support him. His hands went limp and he could do nothing. "You are very kind," he said.

"You are a strange man," she replied, half to herself. "You are an unhappy man."

"Aye . . ." He pulled away from her and began to walk over the turf to the edge of the terrace. Could the Lords of Granbretan know what was going on within him? It was unlikely. It was likely, on the other hand, that they were suspicious and might give the Black Jewel its life at any moment. He took a deep breath of the cold air and straightened his shoulders, remembering the voice of Count Brass from the night before. "Control your thoughts," he had said.

The pain in his head was increasing. He turned. "I think we had better return to the castle," he told Yisselda. She nodded and took his arm again, and they walked back the way they had come.

In the main hall, Count Brass met them. His expression was one of kindly concern, and there was nothing in his face to confirm the urgency of tone Hawkmoon had heard last night. Hawkmoon wondered if he had dreamed that or if Count Brass had guessed the nature of the Black Jewel and was acting to deceive it and the Dark Lords who even now watched this scene from the palace laboratories in Londra.

"The Duke von Köln is feeling unwell," Yisselda said.

"I am distressed to hear it," Count Brass answered. "Is there anything you need, my lord?"

"No," Hawkmoon replied thickly. "No—I thank you." He walked as steadily as he could toward the stairs. Yisselda went with him, supporting one arm, until they reached his rooms. At the door he paused and looked down at her. Her eyes were wide and full of sympathy; she lifted a soft hand to touch his cheek for an instant. The touch sent a shudder through him and he gasped. Then she had turned and half-run down the passage.

Hawkmoon entered the room and flung himself on his bed, his breathing shallow, his body tense, desperately trying to understand what was happening to him and what was the source of the pain in his head. At length he slept again.

He awoke in the afternoon, feeling weak. The pain had nearly gone, and Bowgentle was beside the bed, placing a bowl of fruit on a nearby table. "I was mistaken in believing the fever had left you," he said.

"What is happening to me?" Hawkmoon murmured.

"As far as I can tell, a mild fever brought about by the hardships you have suffered and, I am afraid, by our hospitality. Doubtless it was too soon for you to eat rich food and drink so much wine. We should have realized that. You will be well enough in a short time, however, my lord."

Privately, Hawkmoon knew this diagnosis to be wrong, but he said nothing. He heard a cough to his left and turned his head but saw only the open door leading to the dressing room. Someone was within that room. He looked questioningly back at Bowgentle, but the man's face was blank as he pretended an interest in Hawkmoon's pulse.

"You must not fear," said the voice from the next room. "We wish to help you." The voice was Count Brass's. "We understand the nature of the Jewel in your forehead. When you feel rested, rise and go to the main hall, where Bowgentle will engage you in some sort of trivial conversation. Do not be surprised if his actions seem a little strange."

Bowgentle pursed his lips and straightened up. "You will soon be fit again, my lord. I take my leave of you now."

Hawkmoon watched him leave the room and heard another door close also—Count Brass leaving. How could they have discovered the truth? And how would it affect him? Even now the Dark Lords must be wondering about the odd turn of events and suspecting something. They might release the full life of the Black Jewel at any moment. For some reason, this knowledge disturbed him more.

Hawkmoon decided that there was nothing he could do but obey Count Brass's command, though it was just as likely that the count, if he had discovered the purpose of Hawkmoon's presence here, would be as vengeful as the Lords of Granbretan. Hawkmoon's situation was an unpleasant one in all its possibilities.

When the room darkened and evening came, Hawkmoon got up and walked down to the main hall. It was empty. He looked around him in the flickering firelight, wondering if he had not been induced to enter some sort of trap.

Then Bowgentle came through the far door and smiled at him. He saw Bowgentle's lips move, but no sound came from them. Bowgentle then pretended to pause as if listening to Hawkmoon's reply, and Hawkmoon realized then that this was a deception for the benefit of those who watched through the power of the Black Jewel.

When he heard a footfall behind him, he did not turn, but instead pretended to reply to Bowgentle's conversation.

Then Count Brass spoke from behind him. "We know what the Black Jewel is, my lord Duke. We understand that you were induced by those of Granbretan to come here, and we believe we know the purpose of your visit. I will explain . . ."

Hawkmoon was struck by the oddness of the situation as Bowgentle mimed speech and the count's deep voice came as if from nowhere.

"When you first arrived here at Castle Brass," Count Brass continued, "I realized that the Black Jewel was something more than you said it was—even if you did not yourself realize it. I am afraid that those of the Dark Empire do me little credit, for I have studied quite as much sorcery and science as they, and I have a grimoire in which the machine of the Black Jewel is described. However, I did not know whether you were a knowing or unknowing victim of the Jewel, and I had to discover this without the Granbretanians realizing it.

"Thus on the night of the banquet I asked Sir Bowgentle there to disguise a rune as a pretty set of verses. The purpose of this rune would be to rob you of consciousness—and thus rob the Jewel also—so that we could study you without the Lords of the Dark Empire realizing it. We hoped that they would think you drunk and not connect Bowgentle's pretty rhymes with your own sudden infirmity.

"The rune speaking began, with its special rhythms and cadences designed for your ears. It served its purpose, and you passed into a deep coma. While you slept, Bowgentle and I managed to reach through to your inner mind, which was buried deeply—like a frightened animal that digs a burrow so far underground that it begins to stifle to death. Already certain events had brought your inner mind a little closer to the surface than it had been in Granbretan, and we were able to question it. We discovered most of what had happened to you in Londra, and when I learned of your mission here I almost dispatched you. But then I realized that there was a conflict in you—which even you were scarcely aware of. If this conflict had not been evident, I would have killed you myself or let the Black Jewel do its work."

Hawkmoon, pretending to reply to Bowgentle's non-existent conversation, shuddered in spite of himself.

"However," Count Brass went on, "I realized that you were not to blame for what had occurred and that in killing you I might destroy a potentially powerful enemy of Granbretan. Though I remain neutral, Granbretan has done too much to offend me for me to let such a man die. Thus, we worked out this scheme in order to inform you of what we know and also to say that there is hope. I have the means of temporarily nullifying the power of the Black Jewel. When I have finished, you will accompany Bowgentle down to my chambers, where I will do what must be done. We have little time before the Lords of Granbretan lose patience and release the Jewel's full life into your skull."

Hawkmoon heard Count Brass's footfalls leave the hall, and then Bowgentle smiled and said aloud, "So if you would care to accompany me, my lord, I will show you some parts of the castle you have not as yet visited. Few guests have seen Count Brass's private chambers."

Hawkmoon realized that these words were spoken for the benefit of the watchers in Granbretan. Doubtless Bowgentle was hoping to whet their curiosity and thus gain time.

Bowgentle led the way out of the main hall and into a passage that ended at what appeared to be a solid wall hung with tapestries. Pushing the tapestries aside, Bowgentle touched a small stud set in the stone of the wall, and immediately a section of it began to glow brightly and then faded, to reveal a portal through which, by stooping, a man could pass. Hawkmoon went through, followed by Bowgentle, and found himself in a small room, the walls hung with old charts and diagrams. This room was left and another entered, larger than the first. It contained a great mass of alchemical apparatus and was lined with bookshelves full of huge old volumes of chemistry, sorcery, and philosophy.

"This way," murmured Bowgentle, drawing aside a curtain to reveal a dark passage.

Hawkmoon's eyes strained as he tried to peer through the

darkness, but it was impossible. He stepped cautiously along the passage, and then it was suddenly alive with blinding white light.

Revealed in silhouette was the looming figure of Count Brass, a strangely wrought weapon in his hands pointed at Hawkmoon's head.

Hawkmoon gasped and tried to leap aside, but the passage was too narrow. There was a crack that seemed to burst his eardrums, a weird, melodious humming sound, and he fell back, losing consciousness.

Awakening in golden half light, Hawkmoon had a sense of astonishing physical well-being. His whole mind and body felt alive as if it had never been alive before. He smiled and stretched. He was lying on a metal bench, alone. He reached up and touched his forehead. The Black Jewel was still there, but its texture had changed. No longer did it feel like flesh; no longer did it possess an unnatural warmth. Instead it felt like any ordinary jewel, hard and smooth and cold.

A door opened, and Count Brass entered, looking down at him with an expression of satisfaction.

"I am sorry if I alarmed you yesterday evening," he said, "but I had to work rapidly, paralyzing the Black Jewel and capturing the life force in it. I now possess that life force, imprisoned by means both physical and sorcerous, but I cannot hold it for ever. It is too strong. At some time, it will escape and flow back into the Jewel in your forehead, no matter where you are."

"So I am reprieved but not saved," Hawkmoon said. "How long does the reprieve last?"

"I am not sure. Six months, almost certainly—perhaps a year—perhaps two. But then again, it could be a matter of hours. I cannot deceive you, Dorian Hawkmoon, but I can give you extra hope. There is a sorcerer in the East who could remove the Black Jewel from your head. He is opposed to the Dark Empire and might help you if you could ever find him."

"What is his name?"

"Malagigi of Hamadan."

"Of Persia, then, this sorcerer?"

"Aye," nodded Count Brass. "So far away as to be almost out of your reach."

Hawkmoon sighed and sat up. "Well, then, I must hope your sorcery lasts long enough to sustain me for just a little while. I will leave your lands, Count Brass, and go to Valence to join the army there. It gathers against Granbretan and cannot win, but at least I will take a few of the King-Emperor's dogs with me, by way of vengeance for all they did to me."

Count Brass smiled wryly. "I give you back your life and you immediately decide to sacrifice it. I would suggest that you think for a while before you take any action of any kind. How do you feel, my lord Duke?"

Dorian Hawkmoon swung his legs off the bench and stretched again. "Awake," he said, "a new man . . ." He frowned. "Aye—a new man . . ." he murmured thoughtfully. "And I agree with you, Count Brass. Vengeance can wait until a subtler scheme presents itself."

"In saving you," Count Brass said almost sadly, "I took away your youth. You will never know it again."

6

THE BATTLE OF KAMARG

"They spread neither to east nor west," said Bowgentle one morning some two months later, "but carve their way directly south. There is no doubt, Count Brass, that they realize the truth and plan revenge upon you."

"Perhaps their vengeance is directed at me," Hawkmoon said from where he sat in a deep armchair on one side of the fire. "If I were to go to meet them, they might be satisfied. No doubt they think of me as a traitor."

Count Brass shook his head. "If I know Baron Meliadus, he wants the blood of all of us now. He and his wolves lead the armies. They will not stop until they reach our boundaries."

Von Villach turned from the window where he had been looking out over the town. "Let them come. We will blow them away as the mistral blows the leaves from the trees."

"Let us hope so," said Bowgentle doubtfully. "They have massed their forces. For the first time they seem to have ignored their usual tactics."

"Aye, the fools," muttered Count Brass. "I admired them for the way they spread out in a widening semicircle. That way they could always strengthen their rear before advancing. Now they have unconquered territory on both flanks and enemy armies capable of closing off their rear. If we beat them, they'll have a hard time retreating. Baron Meliadus's vendetta against us robs him of his good sense."

"But if they win," Hawkmoon said softly, "they will have built a road from ocean to ocean, and their conquering will be the easier for that."

"Possibly that is how Meliadus justifies his action," Bowgentle agreed. "I fear he could be right in anticipating such an outcome."

"Nonsense!" von Villach grumbled. "Our towers will resist Granbretan."

"They were designed to withstand an attack from land," Bowgentle pointed out. "We did not reckon for the aerial navies of the Dark Empire."

"We have our own army of the air," Count Brass said.

"The flamingoes are not made of metal," Bowgentle replied.

Hawkmoon rose. He still wore the black leather doublet and breeches given him by Meliadus. The leather creaked as he moved. "Within a few weeks at most, the Dark Empire will be at our door," he said. "What preparations must be made?"

Bowgentle tapped the large map he had rolled under his arm. "First, we should study this."

Count Brass pointed. "Spread it on yonder table."

As Bowgentle spread the map, using wine cups to keep the edges down, Count Brass, von Villach, and Hawkmoon gathered round. The map showed Kamarg and the land surrounding it for some hundred miles.

"They are more or less following the river along its eastern bank," Count Brass said, indicating the Rhone. "From what the messenger said, they should be here"—his finger touched the foothills of the Cevennes—"within a week. We must send out scouts and make sure we know their movements from moment to moment. Then, when they reach our borders, we must have our main force grouped at exactly the right position."

"They might send in their ornithopters ahead," Hawkmoon said. "What then?"

"We'll have our own air scouts circling and be able to anticipate them," von Villach growled. "And the towers will be able to deal with them if the air riders cannot."

"Your actual forces are small," Hawkmoon put in, "so you will be depending heavily on these towers, fighting an almost entirely defensive action."

"That is all we shall need to do," Count Brass told him. "We shall wait at our own borders, with ranks of infantry filling in the spaces between the towers, using heliographers and other signalers to direct the towers to where their power will be most needed."

"We seek only to stop their attack on us," Bowgentle said with a hint of sarcasm. "We have no intention of doing more than withstand them."

Count Brass glanced at him and frowned. "Just so, Bowgentle. We should be fools to press an attack—our few against their many. Our only hope of survival is to depend on the towers and show the King-Emperor and his minions that Kamarg can resist anything he cares to try—whether open battle or long siege—attack from land, sea, or air. To expend men on warfare beyond our borders would be senseless."

"And what say you, friend Hawkmoon?" Bowgentle asked. "You have had experience of battle with the Dark Empire."

Hawkmoon paused, consulting the map. "I see the sense of Count Brass's tactics. I have learned to my cost that any formal battle with Granbretan is out of the question. But it occurs to me that we could weigh the odds further to our advantage if we could pick our own battleground. Where are the defenses strongest?"

Von Villach pointed to an area south-east of the Rhone. "Here, where the towers are thickest and there is high ground where our men could group. At the same time, the ground over which the enemy would have to come is marshy in this season and would cause them some difficulty." He shrugged. "But what point is there in such wishful discussion? They will pick the point of attack, not we."

"Unless they could be *driven* there," Hawkmoon said.

"What would drive them? A storm of knives?" Count Brass smiled.

"I would," Hawkmoon told him. "With the aid of a couple of hundred mounted warriors—never engaging them in open battle, but constantly nibbling at their flanks, we could guide them, with luck, to that spot as your dogs drive your bulls. At the same time, we should have them always in sight and be able to send messages to you so that you would know at all times exactly where they were."

Count Brass rubbed at his moustache and looked at Hawkmoon with some respect. "A tactician after my own heart. Perhaps I'm becoming overcautious, after all, in my old age. If I were younger, I might have conceived a similar scheme. It could work, Hawkmoon, with a great deal of luck."

Von Villach cleared his throat. "Aye—luck and endurance. D'you realize what you're taking on, lad? There'd be scant time for sleeping, you'd have to be on your guard at all hours. It's a grueling task you're considering. Would you be man enough for it? And could the soldiers you take stand it? Then there's the flying machines to consider . . ."

"We'd only need to keep watch for their scouts," Hawkmoon said, "for we'd strike and run before they could get their main force into the air. Your men know the terrain—know where to hide."

Bowgentle pursed his lips. "There's another consideration. The reason they're following the river is to be near their water-carried supplies. They're using the river to bear provisions, spare mounts, war engines, ornithopters—which is why they move so rapidly. How could they be induced to part company with their barges?"

Hawkmoon thought for a moment, then grinned. "Not too difficult a question to answer. Listen . . ."

Next day, Dorian Hawkmoon went riding across the wild marshland, the lady Yisselda at his side. They had spent much time together since his recovery, and he was deeply attached to her, though he seemed to show her little attention. Content enough to be near him, she was yet sometimes piqued that he made no demonstration of affection. She did not know that he wanted nothing more than to do so but that he felt a responsibility toward her that made him control his natural desire to court her. For he knew that at any moment of the night or day he might become in the space of a few minutes a mindless, shambling creature bereft of his humanity. He lived constantly in the knowledge that the Black Jewel's power could burst the bonds Count Brass had cast around it and that shortly afterwards the Lords of Granbretan would give the Jewel its full life and it would eat his mind.

So he did not tell her that he loved her and that this love had first stirred his inner mind from its slumber and that because he saw this, Count Brass had spared his life. And she was, for her part, too shy to tell him of her love.

They rode together over the marshes, feeling the wind in their faces, tugging at their cloaks, galloping faster than was wise through the winding, hidden causeways through the lagoons and swamps, disturbing quail and duck, sending them squawking into the skies, coming upon herds of wild horses and stampeding them, alarming the white bulls and their wives, galloping to the long, lonely beaches where the cold surf spread, splashing through the spray, beneath the shadows of the watchful guard towers, laughing up at the lowering clouds, horses' hoofs beating on the sand, and at length bringing their steeds to a halt to stare out to sea and shout above the song of the mistral.

"You leave tomorrow, Bowgentle tells me," she called, and the wind dropped for a moment and all was suddenly still.

"Aye. Tomorrow." He turned his sad face to her, then quickly turned away again. "Tomorrow. It will not be long before I return."

"Do not be killed, Dorian."

He laughed reassuringly. "It's not my fate, I think, to be killed by Granbretan. If it were—I'd be dead several times over."

She began to reply, but then the wind came roaring in again, catching her hair and curling it about her face. He leaned over to disentangle it, feeling her soft skin and wishing with all his heart that he could hold her face cupped in his hands and touch her lips with his. She reached up to grasp his wrist and keep his hand where it was, but he withdrew it gently, wheeled his horse, and began to ride inland, toward Castle Brass.

The clouds streamed across the sky, above the flattened reeds and the rippling water of the lagoons. A little rain fell, but hardly enough to dampen their shoulders. They rode back slowly, both lost in their own thoughts.

Clad in chain mail from throat to feet, a steel helm with nasals to protect head and face, a long, tapering broadsword at his side, a shield without insignia, Dorian Hawkmoon raised his hand to bring his men to a halt. The men bristled with weapons—bows, slings, some flame-lances, throwing axes, spears—anything that could be hurled from a distance. They were slung across their backs, over their pommels, tied to the sides of their horses, carried in their hands and at their belts. Hawkmoon dismounted and followed his outrider toward the crest of the hill, bending low and moving cautiously.

Reaching the top, he lay on his belly and looked down into the valley where the river wound. It was his first sight of the full might of Granbretan.

It was like a vast legion out of hell, moving slowly southward, battalion upon battalion of marching infantry, squadron after squadron of cavalry, every man masked so that it seemed that the entire animal kingdom marched against Kamarg. Tall banners sprouted from this throng, and metal standards swayed on long poles. There was the banner of Asrovak Mikosevaar, with its grinning, sword-wielding corpse on whose shoulder a vulture perched; beneath it were stitched the words *DEATH TO LIFE!* The tiny figure swaggering in his saddle close to this standard must be Asrovak Mikosevaar himself. Next to Baron Meliadus, he was the most ruthless of all the Warlords of Granbretan. Nearby was the cat standard of Duke Vendel, Grand Constable of that Order, the fly banner of Lord Jerek Nankenseen, and a hundred other similar flags of a hundred other Orders. Even the mantis banner was there, though the Grand Constable was absent—he was the King-Emperor Huon. But in the forefront rode the wolf-masked figure of Meliadus, carrying his own standard, the snarling figure of a rampant wolf; even his horse was caparisoned all in armour with fancifully wrought chamfron resembling the head of a gigantic wolf.

The ground shook, even at this distance, as the army moved on, and through the air came the jingle and clatter of its arms, the stench of sweat and of animals.

Hawkmoon did not look for long at the army proper. He concentrated on the river beyond, noting the vast numbers of heavily laden barges that lay side by side, so thick that they almost hid the water. He smiled and whispered to the scout at his side, "It suits our plan, you see? All their watercraft bunched together. Come, we must circle their army and get a good distance behind it."

They ran back down the hill. Hawkmoon climbed into his saddle and waved for his men to move on. Following him, they rode at speed, knowing there was little time to spare.

They rode for the best part of that day until the army of Granbretan was merely a cloud of dust to the south and the river was free of the Dark Empire's ships. Here the Rhone narrowed and became shallow, running through an artificial watercourse of ancient stone, with a low stone bridge spanning it. The ground on one side was flat, and on the other it sloped gently down to form a valley.

Wading through this part of the river as evening came, Hawkmoon looked carefully at the stone banks, looked up at the bridge, and tested the nature of the river bed itself while water rushed around his legs, chilling them as it crept between the links of his mail stockings. The watercourse was in poor condition. It had been built before the Tragic Millennium and hardly repaired since. It had been used to divert the river for some reason. Now Hawkmoon intended to put it to a new use.

On the bank, waiting for his signal, were grouped his flame-lancers, holding their long, unwieldy weapons carefully. Hawkmoon climbed back to the bank and began pointing out certain spots on the bridge and the banks. The flame-lancers saluted and began to move in the directions he had indicated, raising their weapons. Hawkmoon stretched his arm toward the west, where the ground fell away, and called to them. They nodded.

As the sky darkened, red flame began to roar from the tapering snouts of the weapons, cut its way into stone, turned water into boiling steam, until all was heat and tumbling chaos.

Through the night, the flame-lances did their work; then sud-

denly there was a great groan and the bridge collapsed into the
river in a great cloud of spray, sending scalding water in all directions. Now the flame-lancers turned their attention to the western
bank, carving out blocks that tumbled down into the dammed
river, which was beginning to spread out around the bridge that
blocked it.

By morning, water rushed down a new course into the valley,
and only a small stream flowed along the original bed.

Tired but satisfied, Hawkmoon and his men grinned at one
another and mounted their horses, turning away in the direction
whence they had come. They had struck their first blow against
Granbretan. And it was an effective blow.

Hawkmoon and his soldiers rested in the hills for a few hours and
then went to look at the Dark Empire's army again.

Hawkmoon smiled as he lay beneath the cover of a bush and
looked down into the valley at the scene of confusion there.

The river was now a morass of dark mud, and in it, like so
many stranded whales, lay the battle barges of Granbretan, some
with prows jutting high and sterns buried deep in the stuff of
the river bed, some on their sides, some bow-first in the mud,
some upside-down, war engines scattered, livestock in panic, provisions ruined. And wading among all this the soldiers attempted
to haul the mud-encrusted cargoes to land, free horses from their
entangling ropes and straps, and rescue sheep, pigs, and cows that
struggled wildly in the morass.

There was a great noise of bellowing animals and shouting
men. The uniform ranks that Hawkmoon had seen earlier were

now broken. On the banks, proud cavalrymen were being forced to use their horses like dray animals to haul barges closer to firm ground. Elsewhere, camps had been erected as Meliadus had realized the impossibility of moving on until the cargoes were rescued. Although guards had been posted around the camps, their attention was on the river and not on the hills where Hawkmoon and his men waited.

It was coming close to dark, and since the ornithopters could not fly at night, Baron Meliadus would not know the exact reason for the river's sudden drying up until the next day. Then, Hawkmoon reasoned, he would dispatch engineers upriver to try to put right the damage; but Hawkmoon was prepared for this.

Now it was time to ready his men. He crept back down to the depression in the hillside where his soldiers were bivouacked and began to confer with his captains. He had a particular objective in view, one he hoped might help demoralize the warriors of Granbretan.

Nightfall, and by the light of brands the men in the valley continued their work, manhandling the heavy war engines to the bank, dragging cases of provisions up the steep sides of the river bed. Meliadus, whose impatience to reach Kamarg allowed his men no rest, rode among the weary, sweating soldiers urging them on. Behind him, each great circle of tents surrounded the particular standard of its Order, but few of the tents were fully occupied since most of the forces were still at work.

No-one saw the approaching shapes of the mounted warriors

whose horses walked softly down from the hills, each man swathed in a dark cloak.

Hawkmoon drew his horse to a halt, and his right hand went to his left side, where the fine sword Meliadus had given him was scabbarded. He swept the sword out, raised it for a moment, then pointed it forward. It was the signal to charge.

Without warcries, their only sound the thunder of their horses' hoofs and the clank of their accoutrements, the Kamargians plunged forward, led by Hawkmoon, who leaned across his horse's neck and made straight for a surprised guard. His sword took the man in the throat, and with a gurgling murmur the guard collapsed. Through the first of the tents they went, slashing at guy ropes, cutting down the few armed men who tried to stop them, and still the Granbretanians had no idea who attacked them. Hawkmoon reached the centre of the first circle, and his sword swung in a great arc as he chopped at the standard that stood there—the standard of the Order of the Hound. The pole cracked, groaned, and fell into a cooking fire, sending up a great shower of sparks.

Hawkmoon did not pause; he urged his horse on into the heart of the huge camp. On the riverbank there was no alarm, for the invaders could not be heard over the din the Granbretanians themselves made.

Three half-armoured swordsmen ran toward Hawkmoon. He yanked his horse sideways and swung his broadsword left and right, meeting their blades and striking one from its owner's hand. The other two pressed in, but Hawkmoon chopped at a wrist, severing it. The remaining warrior backed away, and Hawkmoon lunged at him, his sword piercing the man's breast.

The horse reared, and Hawkmoon fought to control it, forcing it through another line of tents, his men following. He broke out across an open space, to see his way blocked by a group of warriors dressed only in nightshirts and armed with swords and bucklers. Hawkmoon shouted an order to his horsemen, and they spread out to charge full tilt at the line, their swords held straight before them. Almost in a single movement they killed or knocked flying the line of warriors and were through into the next circle of tents, guy ropes twisting in the air as they were cut, tents collapsing upon their occupants.

At last, his sword glistening with blood, Hawkmoon fought his way to the centre of this circle, and there stood what he sought— the proud mantis banner of the Order of which the King-Emperor himself was Grand Constable. A band of warriors stood round it, pulling on helmets and adjusting their shields on their arms. Without waiting to see if his men followed, Hawkmoon thundered toward them with a wild yell. A shiver ran up his arm as his sword clanged against the shield of the nearest warrior, but he lifted it again, and the sword split the shield, gashing the face of the man behind it so that he reeled back, spitting blood from his ruined mouth. Another Hawkmoon took in the side, and another's head was shorn off clean. His blade rose and fell like some relentless machine, and now his men joined him, pressing the warriors farther and farther back into a tighter and tighter ring about the mantis banner.

Hawkmoon's mail was ripped by a sword-stroke, his shield was struck from his arm, but he fought on until only one man stood by the banner.

Hawkmoon grinned, leaned forward, tipped the man's helmet

off his head with a movement of his sword, and clove the skull in twain. Then he reached out and yanked the mantis banner from the earth, raised it high to display it to his cheering men, and turned his horse about, riding for the hills again, the steed leaping corpses and tangled tents with ease.

He heard a wounded warrior yell from behind him, "Did you see him? He has a Black Jewel embedded in his skull!"—and he knew that before long Baron Meliadus would understand who had raided his camp and stolen his army's most precious standard.

Hawkmoon turned in the direction of the shout, shook the banner triumphantly, and laughed a wild, mocking laugh.

"Hawkmoon!" he cried. "Hawkmoon!" It was the age-old battleshout of his forefathers. It sprang unconsciously to his lips now, bidden by his will to let his great enemy Meliadus, the slayer of his kin, know who opposed him.

The coal-black stallion on which he rode reared up, red nostrils flaring, eyes glaring, was wheeled around on its hindlegs, and plunged through the confusion of the camp.

Behind them came mounted warriors, hastily riding in pursuit, goaded on by Hawkmoon's infuriating laughter.

Hawkmoon and his men soon reached the hills again and headed for the secret encampment they had already prepared. Behind them blundered Meliadus's men. Looking back, Hawkmoon saw that the scene on the dried-up riverbank had turned into even greater confusion. Torches moved hurriedly toward the camp.

Knowing the country as they did, Hawkmoon's men had soon

outdistanced their pursuers and at length come to a rocky hillside where they had camouflaged a cave entrance the previous day. Into this cave they now rode, dismounting and replacing the camouflage. The cave was large, and there were even larger caverns beyond it, big enough to take their whole force and stable their horses. A small stream ran through the farthest cave, which held provisions for several days. Other secret camps had been prepared all the way back to Kamarg.

Someone lit brands, and Hawkmoon dismounted, hefting the mantis standard and flinging it into a corner. He grinned at round-faced Pelaire, his chief lieutenant.

"Tomorrow Meliadus will send engineers back to our dam, once his ornithopters have reported. We must make sure they do not destroy our handiwork."

Pelaire nodded. "Aye, but even if we slay one party, he'll send another . . ."

Hawkmoon shrugged. "And another, doubtless—but I rely upon his impatience to reach Kamarg. At length he should realize the pointlessness in wasting time and men in trying to redivert the river. Then he will press on—and with luck, if we survive, we should be able to drive him south-east to our borders."

Pelaire had begun to count the numbers of the returning warriors. Hawkmoon waited until he had finished, then asked, "What losses?"

Pelaire's face was a mixture of elation and disbelief. "None, master—we have not lost a man!"

"A good omen," Hawkmoon said, slapping Pelaire on the back. "Now we must rest, for we have a long ride in the morning."

At dawn, the guard they had left at the entrance came back to report bad news.

"A flying machine," he told Hawkmoon as the duke washed himself in the stream. "It has been circling above for the last ten minutes."

"Do you think the pilot has guessed something—made out our tracks, perhaps?" Pelaire put in.

"Impossible," Hawkmoon said, drying his face. "The rock would show nothing even to someone on the ground. We must bide our time—those ornithopters cannot remain airborne for long without returning to re-power."

But an hour later the guard returned to say that a second ornithopter had arrived to replace the first. Hawkmoon bit his lip, then reached a decision. "Time is running out. Before the engineers can begin work we must get to the dam. We shall have to resort to a riskier plan than I'd hoped to use . . ."

Swiftly he drew one of his men aside and spoke to him; then he gave orders for two flame-lancers to come forward, and, last, he told the rest of his men to saddle their horses and be prepared to leave the cavern.

A little later, a single horseman rode out of the cavern entrance and began slowly to ride down the gentle, rocky slope.

Watching from the cave. Hawkmoon saw the sun glance off the body of the great, brazen flying machine as its mechanical wings flapped noisily in the air and it began to descend toward the lone man. Hawkmoon had counted on the pilot's curiosity.

Now he made a gesture with his hand, and the flame-lancers brought their long, unwieldy weapons up, their ruby coils already beginning to glow in readiness. The disadvantages of the flame-lance were that it could not be operated instantly and it often grew too hot to hold easily.

Now the ornithopter was circling lower and lower. The hidden flame-lancers raised their weapons. The pilot could be seen, leaning over his cockpit, crow-mask peering downward.

"Now," murmured Hawkmoon.

As one, the red lines of flame left the tips of the lances. The first splashed against the side of the ornithopter and merely heated the armour a little. But the second struck the pilot's body, which almost instantly began to flare. The pilot beat at his burning garments, and his hands left the delicate controls of the machine. The wings flapped erratically, and the ornithopter twisted in the air, keeled to one side, and plunged earthward with the pilot trying to bring the flying machine out of its dive. It struck a nearby hillside and crumpled to pieces, the wings still beating for an instant, the pilot's broken body flung some yards away; then it burst apart with a strange smacking sound. It did not catch fire, but the pieces were scattered widely over the hillside. Hawkmoon did not understand the peculiarities of the power unit used for the ornithopters, but one of them was the manner in which it exploded.

Hawkmoon mounted the black stallion and signaled his men to follow him. Within moments they were galloping down the rocky slope of the hill, heading for the dam they had made the day before.

The winter's day was bright and clear, and the air was exhilarating. They rode with some confidence, cheered by their success of last night. They slowed down, eventually, when the dam was close, saw the river flowing on its new course, watched from the top of the hill as a detachment of warriors and engineers inspected the broken bridge that successfully blocked the water from its earlier course, and then charged down, the mounted flame-lancers in the lead, leaning back in their stirrups while they operated their temperamental weapons.

Ten lines of fire poured toward the surprised Granbretanians, turning men into living brands that ran screaming for the water. Fire swept across the ranks of men in the masks of mole and badger and the protecting force in their vulture masks—Asrovak Mikosevaar's mercenaries. Then Hawkmoon's men had clashed with them, and the air rang with the clangour of their weapons. Bloody axes swung in the air, swords swept back and forth, men screamed in death agonies, horses snorted and whinnied with hoofs flailing.

Hawkmoon's horse, protected by chain armour, staggered as a huge man swung a great double-bladed war-axe at it. The horse fell, dragging Hawkmoon down, its body trapping him. The vulture-masked axeman moved in, raising the weapon over Hawkmoon's face. Hawkmoon pulled his arm from beneath the horse, and there was a sword in his hand that swept up just in time to take the main force of the blow. The horse was clambering to its feet again. Hawkmoon sprang up and grabbed its reins while at the same time protecting himself from the swinging axe.

Once, twice, thrice, the weapons met, until Hawkmoon's sword arm ached. Then he slid his blade down the shaft and struck the axeman's fists. Hawkmoon's adversary let go of the weapon with one hand, a muffled oath coming from within the mask. Hawkmoon smashed his sword against the metal mask, denting it. The man groaned and staggered. Hawkmoon got both hands on the grip of the broadsword and brought the blade around to chop deep into the head again. The vulture mask split, and a bloodied face was revealed, the bearded mouth screaming for mercy. Hawkmoon's eyes narrowed, for he loathed the mercenaries more than he loathed the Granbretanians. He delivered a third blow to the head, staving in all of one side so that the man waltzed backward, already dead, and crumpled against one of his fellows who was engaged with a Kamargian horseman.

Hawkmoon remounted and led his men against the last of the Vulture Legion, hacking and thrusting in a fever of bloodletting, until only the engineers, armed with short swords, remained. These presented little opposition and were shortly all slain, their bodies strewn across the dam and drifting down the river they had sought to redivert.

Pelaire glanced at Hawkmoon as they rode away toward the hills. "You have no mercy in you, captain!"

"Aye," Hawkmoon replied distantly, "none. Man, woman, or child, if they be of or for Granbretan, they are my enemies to be slain."

Eight of their number were dead. Considering the strength of the force they had destroyed, they had again known great luck. The Granbretanians were used to massacring their enemies, they were not used to being attacked in this manner. Perhaps this explained the few losses the men of Kamarg had suffered so far.

Four more expeditions Meliadus sent to destroy the dam, each expedition of increasing numbers. Each was destroyed in turn by sudden attacks from the horsemen of Kamarg, and of the original two hundred riders who followed Dorian Hawkmoon, nearly a hundred and fifty remained to carry out the second part of his plan and harry the armies of Granbretan so that they turned slowly, encumbered as they were by their land-borne war engines and supplies, toward the south-east.

Hawkmoon never afterward attacked by day, when the ornithopters circled the skies, but would creep in by night. His flame-lances burned scores of tents and their occupants, his arrows cut down dozen upon dozen of the men assigned to guard the tents and the warriors who went out by day to seek for the Kamargians' secret camps. Swords scarcely dried before they were wetted again, axes became blunt with their deadly work, and heavy Kamarg spears were in short supply among their original owners. Hawkmoon and his men became haggard and red-eyed, hardly able to keep their saddles at times, often coming within a hairsbreadth of discovery by the ornithopters or search parties. They ensured that the road from the river was lined with Granbretanian corpses—and that that road was the one they chose for the Dark Empire forces to tread.

As Hawkmoon had guessed, Meliadus did not spend the time he should trying to seek out the guerilla riders. His impatience to reach Kamarg dominated even his great hatred for Hawkmoon, and doubtless he reasoned that once he had vanquished Kamarg there would be time enough to deal with Hawkmoon.

Once and only once they came close to confronting one another, as Hawkmoon and his riders moved among the tents and cooking fires, stabbing at random and preparing to leave, since dawn was close. Meliadus, mounted, came up with a group of his wolf cavalry, saw Hawkmoon butchering a couple of men entangled in a fallen tent, and charged toward him.

Hawkmoon looked up, raised his sword to meet Meliadus's, and smiled grimly, pushing the sword gradually backward.

Meliadus grunted as Hawkmoon forced his arm farther and farther back.

"My thanks, Baron Meliadus," said Hawkmoon. "The nurturing you gave me in Londra seems to have improved my strength . . ."

"Oh, Hawkmoon," Meliadus replied, his voice soft but shaking with rage, "I know not how you escaped the power of the Black Jewel, but you will suffer a fate many thousand times greater than the one you have avoided when I take Kamarg and once again make you my prisoner."

Suddenly Hawkmoon moved his blade in under the brass quillons of Meliadus's sword, turned the point, and sent the other's weapon spinning away. He raised the broadsword to strike, then realized that too many Granbretanians were coming up.

"Time to be away, Baron, I regret. I'll remember your promise—when you're my prisoner!"

He wheeled his horse about and, laughing, was away, leading his men out of the chaos that was the camp. With an angry motion of his hand, Meliadus dismounted to retrieve his sword. "Upstart!" he swore. "He'll crawl at my feet before the month is past."

The day came when Hawkmoon and his riders made no further attacks on Meliadus's forces but galloped swiftly through the marshy ground that lay below the line of hills where Count Brass, Leopold von Villach, and their army awaited them. The tall, dark towers, almost as ancient as Kamarg itself, loomed over the scene, packed now with more than one guardian, snouts of bizarre weapons jutting from almost every slit.

Hawkmoon's horse climbed the hill, approaching the solitary figure of Count Brass, who smiled with great warmth and relief when he recognized the young nobleman.

"I am glad I decided to let you live, Duke von Köln," he said humourously. "You have done everything you planned—and kept the best part of your force alive. I'm not sure I could have done better myself, in my prime."

"Thank you, Count Brass. Now we must prepare. Baron Meliadus is hardly half a day's march behind us."

Below him now, on the far side of the hill, he could see the Kamargian force, primarily infantry, drawn up.

At most a thousand men, they looked pitifully few compared with the vast weight of warriors marching to meet them. The Kamargians were outnumbered at least twenty to one, probably by twice that amount.

Count Brass saw Hawkmoon's expression.

"Do not fear, lad. We have better weapons than swords with which to resist this invasion."

Hawkmoon had been mistaken in thinking Granbretan would reach the borders in half a day. They had decided to camp before marching on, and it was not until noon of the following day that the Kamargians saw the force approach, moving over the flat plain in a spread-out formation. Each square of infantry and cavalry was made up of a particular Order, each member of the Order pledged to defend every other member whether that member was alive or dead. This system was part of Granbretan's great strength, for it meant that no man ever retreated unless specifically ordered to do so by his Grand Constable.

Count Brass sat on his horse and watched the enemy approach. On one side of him was Dorian Hawkmoon, on the other Leopold von Villach. Here, it was Count Brass who would give the orders. *Now the battle begins in earnest*, thought Hawkmoon, and it was hard to see how they could win. Was Count Brass overconfident?

The mighty concourse of fighting men and machines came eventually to a halt about half a mile away; then two figures broke from the main body and began to ride toward the hill. As they came closer, Hawkmoon recognized the standard as that of Baron Meliadus and realized a moment later that one of the figures was Meliadus himself, riding with his herald. He held a bronze megaphone, symbolizing the wish for a peaceful parley.

"Surely he can't wish to surrender—or expect us to," von Villach said in a tone of disgruntlement.

"I would think not," smiled Hawkmoon. "Doubtless this is one of his tricks. He is famous for them."

Noting the quality of Hawkmoon's smile, Count Brass counseled, "Be wary of that hatred, Dorian Hawkmoon. Do not let it possess your reason the way it possesses Meliadus's."

Hawkmoon stared straight in front of him and did not reply.

Now the herald lifted the heavy megaphone to his lips.

"I speak for Baron Meliadus, Grand Constable of the Order of the Wolf, First Chieftain of the Armies under the most noble

King-Emperor Huon, ruler of Granbretan and destined ruler of all Europe."

"Tell your master to lift his mask and speak for himself," Count Brass called back.

"My master offers you honourable peace. If you surrender now, he promises that he will slay nobody and will merely appoint himself as Governor of your province in King Huon's name, to see justice done and order brought to this unruly land. We offer you mercy. If you refuse, all Kamarg will be laid waste, everything shall be burned and the sea let in to flood what remains. The Baron Meliadus says that you well know it is in his power to do all this and that your resistance will be the cause of the deaths of your kin as well as yourselves."

"Tell Baron Meliadus, who hides behind his mask, too abashed to speak since he knows that he is a graceless cur who has abused my hospitality and been beaten by me in a fair fight—tell your master that we may well be the death of him and all his kind. Tell him that he is a cowardly dog and a thousand of his ilk could not bring down one of our Kamarg bulls. Tell him that we sneer at his offer of peace as a trick—a deception that could be seen for what it is by a child. Tell him that we need no governor, that we govern ourselves to our own satisfaction. Tell him . . ."

Count Brass broke into a jeering laugh as Baron Meliadus angrily turned his horse about and, with the herald at his heels, galloped back toward his men.

They waited for a quarter of an hour, and then they saw the ornithopters rise into the air. Hawkmoon sighed. He had been defeated once by the flying machines. Would he be defeated for a second time?

Count Brass raised his sword in a signal, and there was a great flapping and snapping sound. Looking behind him, Hawkmoon saw the scarlet flamingoes sweeping upward, their graceful flight exceedingly beautiful in comparison with the clumsy motions of the metal ornithopters that parodied them. Soaring into the sky, the scarlet flamingoes, with their riders in their high saddles, each man armed with a flame-lance, wheeled toward the brazen ornithopters.

Gaining height, the flamingoes were in the better position, but it was hard to believe that they would be a match for the machines of metal, however clumsy. Red streamers of flame, hardly visible from this distance, struck the sides of the ornithopters, and one pilot was hit, killed almost instantly and falling from his machine. The pilotless ornithopter flapped on; then its wings folded behind it and it plunged downward, to land, birdlike, prow first, in the swamp below the hill. Hawkmoon saw an ornithopter fire its twin flame cannon at a flamingo and its rider, and the scarlet bird leaped in the air, somersaulted, and crashed to earth in a great shower of feathers. The air was hot and the flying machines noisy, but Count Brass's attention was now on the Granbretanian cavalry, which was advancing toward the hill at a charge.

Count Brass made no movement at first; he merely watched the huge press of horsemen as they came nearer and nearer. Then he lifted his sword again, yelling: "Towers—open fire!"

The nozzles of some of the unfamiliar weapons turned toward the enemy riders, and there came a shrieking sound that Hawkmoon thought would split his head, but he saw nothing come from the weapons. Then he saw that the horses were rearing, just as they reached the swampland. Every one was bucking now, eyes

rolling and foam flecking its lips. Riders were flung off until half the cavalry was crawling in the swamp, slipping on the treacherous mud, trying to control their animals.

Count Brass turned to Hawkmoon. "A weapon that emits an invisible beam down which sound travels. You heard a little of it—the horses experienced its full intensity."

"Shall we charge them now?" Hawkmoon asked.

"No—no need. Wait, curb your impatience."

The horses were falling, stiff and senseless. "It kills them, unfortunately, in the end," Count Brass said.

Soon all the horses lay in the mud while their riders cursed and waded back to firm ground, standing there uncertainly.

Above them, flamingoes dived and circled around the ornithopters, making up in grace for what they lacked in power and strength. But many of the giant birds were falling—more than the ornithopters, with their clanking wings and whirring engines.

Great stones began to crash down near the towers.

"The war machines—they're using their catapults," von Villach growled. "Can't we . . . ?"

"Patience," said Count Brass, apparently unperturbed.

Then a great wave of heat struck them, and they saw a huge funnel of crimson fire splash against the nearest tower. Hawkmoon pointed. "A fire cannon—the largest I've ever seen. It will destroy us all!"

Count Brass was riding for the tower under attack. They saw him leap from his horse and enter the building, which seemed doomed. Moments later the tower began to spin faster and faster, and Hawkmoon realized in astonishment that it was disappearing below the ground, the flame passing harmlessly over it. The cannon turned its attention to the next tower, and as it did so, this tower began to spin and retreat into the ground while the first tower whirled upward again, came to a halt, and let fire at the flame cannon with a weapon mounted on the battlements. This weapon shone green and purple and had a bell-shaped mouth. A series of round white objects flew from it and landed near the flame cannon. Hawkmoon could see them bouncing amongst the engineers who manned the weapon. Then his attention was diverted as an ornithopter crashed close by and he was forced to turn his horse and gallop along the crest of the hill until he was out of range of the exploding power unit. Von Villach joined him. "What are those things?" Hawkmoon asked, but von Villach shook his head, as puzzled as his comrade.

Then Hawkmoon saw that the white spheres had stopped bouncing and that the flame cannon no longer gouted fire. Also the hundred or so people near the cannon were no longer moving. Hawkmoon realized with a shock that they were frozen. More of the white spheres shot from the bell-shaped mouth of the weapon and bounced near the catapults and other war engines of Granbretan. Shortly, the crews of these were also frozen and rocks ceased to fall near the towers.

Count Brass left the tower he had entered and rode back to join them. He was grinning. "We have still other weapons to display to these fools," he said.

"But can they fight such a weight of men?" Hawkmoon asked, for the infantry were now moving forward, their numbers so vast that it seemed not even the mightiest weapons could stop their advance.

"We shall see," Count Brass replied, signaling to a lookout on a nearby tower. The air above them was black with fighting birds and machines, red traceries of fire criss-crossing the sky, pieces of metal and bloody feathers falling all around them. It was impossible to tell which side was winning.

The infantry was almost upon them when Count Brass waved his sword to the lookout and the tower turned wide-muzzled weapons toward the armies of Granbretan. Glass spheres, shimmering blue in the light, hurtled toward the advancing warriors and fell among them. Hawkmoon saw them break formation, begin to run about wildly, flailing at the air and ripping off the masks of their respective Orders.

"What has happened?" he asked Count Brass in amazement.

"The spheres contain a hallucinatory gas," Count Brass told him. "It makes the men see dreadful visions." Now he turned in his saddle and waved his sword to the waiting men below. They began to advance. "The time has come to meet Granbretan with ordinary weapons," he said.

From the remaining ranks of infantry, arrows flew thickly toward them and flame-lances sent searing fire. Count Brass's archers retaliated, and his flame-lancers also returned the attack. Arrows clattered on their armour. Several men fell. Others were struck down by the flame-lances. Through the chaos of fire and flying arrows, the infantry of Granbretan steadily advanced, in spite of depleted numbers. They paused when they came to the swampy ground, choked as it was with the bodies of their horses, and their officers furiously urged them on.

Count Brass ordered his herald forward, and the man approached, bearing the simple flag of his master—a red gauntlet on a white field.

The three men waited as the infantry broke ranks and began to clamber through the mud and over the corpses of the horses, struggling to reach the hill where the forces of Kamarg waited to meet them.

Hawkmoon saw Meliadus some distance in the rear and recognized the barbaric vulture-mask of Asrovak Mikosevaar as the Muskovian led his Vulture Legion on foot and was one of the first to cross the swamp and reach the slopes of the hill.

Hawkmoon trotted his horse forward a little so that he would be directly in the path of Mikosevaar when he approached.

He heard a bellow, and the vulture-mask glared at him with eyes of ruby. "Aha! Hawkmoon! The dog that has worried at us for so long! Now let's see how you conduct yourself in a fair fight, traitor!"

"Call me not 'traitor,'" Hawkmoon said angrily. "You sniffer of corpses!"

Mikosevaar hefted his great war axe in his armoured hands, bellowed again, and began to run toward Hawkmoon, who jumped from his horse and, with shield and broadsword, prepared to defend himself.

The axe, shod all in metal, thundered against the shield and sent Hawkmoon staggering back a pace. Another blow followed and split the top edge of the shield. Hawkmoon swung his sword around, and it struck Mikosevaar's heavily armoured shoulder with a great ringing sound, sending up a shower of sparks. Both men held their ground, giving blow for blow as the battle raged around them. Hawkmoon glanced at von Villach and saw him engaged with Mygel Holst, Archduke of Londra, well-matched in age and strength, and Count Brass was ploughing through the lesser warriors, trying to seek out Meliadus, who had plainly decided to supervise the battle from a distance.

From their advantageous position, the Kamargians withstood the Dark Empire warriors, holding their line firm.

Hawkmoon's shield was a ruin of jagged metal and useless. He flung it from his arm and seized his sword in both hands, swinging it to meet the blow Mikosevaar aimed at his head. The two men grunted with exertion as they maneuvered about in the slippery earth of the hill, now jabbing to try to make the other lose his footing, now slashing suddenly at the legs or torso or battering from above or the side.

Hawkmoon was sweating heavily in his armour, and he grunted with effort. Then suddenly his foot slid from under him and he fell to one knee, Mikosevaar lumbering forward to raise his axe and decapitate his enemy. Hawkmoon flung himself flat, toward Mikosevaar, and grabbed at the man's legs, pulling him down so that both men rolled over and over toward the swamp and the mounds of dead horses.

Punching and cursing, they came to a halt in the filth. Neither had lost his weapon, and now they stumbled to their feet, preparing to continue the fight. Hawkmoon braced himself against the body of a warhorse and swung at the Muskovian. The swing would have broken Mikosevaar's neck had not he ducked, but it knocked the vulture helm from his head, revealing the white, bushy beard and glaring, insane eyes of the Muskovian, who brought his axe upward toward Hawkmoon's belly and had the blow blocked by the sword whistling down.

Releasing his grip on the sword, Hawkmoon pushed with

both hands at Mikosevaar's chest, and the man fell backward. As he tried to scramble up, Hawkmoon took a fresh hold of his broadsword, raised it high, and plunged it at the Muskovian's face. The man yelled. The blade rose and descended again. Asrovak Mikosevaar shrieked, and then the sound was suddenly cut off. Hawkmoon lost interest in the groaning thing at his feet and turned to see how the battle went.

It was hard to tell. Everywhere men were falling, and it seemed that the great majority were Granbretanians. The fight in the air was almost over, and only a few ornithopters circled the sky, while there seemed to be many more flamingoes.

Was it possible that Kamarg was winning?

Hawkmoon turned as two warriors of the Vulture Legion ran toward him. Recklessly he stooped to drag up the bloodied mask of Mikosevaar. He laughed at them. "Look! Your Grand Constable is slain—your warlord is destroyed!" The warriors hesitated, then backed away from Hawkmoon and began to run the way they had come. The Vulture Legion did not have the discipline of the other Orders.

Hawkmoon began to clamber wearily over the bodies of the dead horses, which were now liberally heaped with human corpses. The battle was thin in this area, but he could see von Villach on the hill, kicking the wounded body of Mygel Holst and roaring in triumph as he turned to deal with a group of Holst's warriors who ran at him with spears. Von Villach seemed to need no aid. Hawkmoon began to run as best he could up to the top of the hill, to get a better idea of how the battle turned.

His broadsword was blooded thrice before he could reach his

objective and look at the field. The huge army that Meliadus had brought against them was now scarcely a sixth of its former size, while the line of Kamargian warriors still held fast.

Half the banners of the warlords were down, and others were sorely beset. The tight formations of the Granbretanian infantry were largely broken, and Hawkmoon saw that the unprecedented was happening and that the Orders were becoming mixed together, thus throwing their members in confusion, since they were used to fighting side by side with their own brothers.

Hawkmoon saw Count Brass, still mounted, engaged with several swordsmen down the hill. He saw the standard of Meliadus some distance away. It was surrounded by men of the Order of the Wolf. Meliadus had protected himself well. Now Hawkmoon saw several of the commanders—Adaz Promp and Jerek Nankenseen among them—ride toward Meliadus. Evidently they wanted to retreat but must wait for Meliadus's order to do so.

He could guess what the commanders told Meliadus—that the flower of their warriors was being destroyed, that such destruction was not worth suffering for the sake of one tiny province.

But no call came from the trumpets of the heralds who waited nearby. Meliadus was evidently resisting their pleas.

Von Villach came up, riding a borrowed horse. He pushed back his helm and grinned at Hawkmoon. "We're beating them, I think," he said. "Where is Count Brass?"

Hawkmoon pointed. "He is making good account," he smiled. "Should we hold steady or begin to advance—we could if we wished it. I think the Granbretanian warlords are faltering and want to retreat. A push now, and it might make up their minds for them."

Von Villach nodded. "I'll send a messenger down to the count. He must decide."

He turned to a horseman and muttered a few words to him. The man began to race down the hillside, through the confusion of embattled warriors.

Hawkmoon saw him reach the count, saw Count Brass glance up and wave to them, wheel his horse, and begin to return.

Within ten minutes, Count Brass had managed to regain the hill. "Five warlords I slew," he said with a satisfied air. "But Meliadus slunk away."

Hawkmoon repeated what he had said to von Villach, Count Brass agreed with the sense of the plan, and soon the Kamarg infantry began to advance steadily, pushing the Granbretanians down the hill before them.

Hawkmoon found a fresh horse and led the advance, yelling wildly as he chopped about him, striking heads from necks, limbs from torsos, like apples from the bough. His body was covered from head to foot in the blood of the slain. His mail was ragged and threatening to fall from him. His whole chest was a mass of bruises and minor cuts, his arm bled, and his leg ached horribly, but he ignored it all as the bloodlust seized him and he killed man after man.

Riding beside him, von Villach said in a moment of comparative peace, "You seem decided to kill more of the dogs than the rest of our army put together."

"I would not cease if the blood of Granbretan filled this whole plain," Hawkmoon replied grimly. "I would not cease until everything that lived of Granbretan was destroyed."

"Your bloodlust matches theirs," von Villach said ironically.

"Mine is greater," Hawkmoon called, driving forward, "for half theirs is sport."

And, butchering, on he rode.

At last it seemed that his commanders convinced him, for Meliadus's trumpets shouted the retreat and the survivors broke away from the Kamargians and began to run.

Hawkmoon struck down several who threw away their weapons in attitudes of surrender. "I do not care for *living* Granbretanians," he said once as he stabbed a man who had ripped his mask from his young face and begged for mercy.

But at length even Hawkmoon's bitterness was satiated for a while, and he drew up his horse beside those of Count Brass and von Villach and watched as the Granbretanians re-formed their ranks and began to march away.

Hawkmoon thought he heard a great scream of rage rise from the retreating army, thought he recognized the vengeful sound as that of Meliadus, and he smiled.

"We shall see Meliadus again," he said.

Count Brass nodded agreement. "He has found Kamarg invincible to attack by his armies, and he knows that we are too clever to be deceived by his treachery, but he will find some other way. Soon all the lands about Kamarg will belong to the Dark Empire and we shall have to be on our guard the whole time."

When they returned to Castle Brass that night, Bowgentle spoke to the count. "Now do you realize that Granbretan is insane—a cancer that will infect history and will set it on a course that will not only lead to the destruction of the entire human race, but will

ultimately result in the destruction of every intelligent or potentially intelligent creature in the universe?"

Count Brass smiled. "You are exaggerating, Bowgentle. How
could you know so much?"

"Because it is my calling to understand the forces that go to
work to make up what we call destiny. I tell you again, Count
Brass, the Dark Empire will infect the universe unless it is checked
on this planet—and preferably on this continent."

Hawkmoon sat with his legs stretched out before him, doing
his best to work the ache from his muscles. "I have no under-
standing of the philosophical principles you base your beliefs
upon, Sir Bowgentle," he said, "but instinctively I know you to be
right. All we think we see is an implacable enemy that means to
rule the world—there have been other races like them in the
past—but there is something different about the Dark Empire.
Forget you not, Count Brass, that I spent time in Londra and was
witness to many of their more excessive insanities. You have seen
only their armies, which, like most armies, fight fiercely and to
win, using conventional tactics because they are the best. But
there is little conventional about the King-Emperor, immortal
corpse that he is, in his Throne Globe; little conventional about the
secret way they have with one another, the sense of insanity that
underlies the mood of the entire city . . ."

"You think we have not, then, witnessed the worst of what
they can do?" Count Brass asked seriously.

"That is what I think," Hawkmoon said. "It is not only the
need for vengeance that makes me slay them as I do—it is a
deeper thing within me that sees them as a threat to the forces of
Life itself."

Count Brass sighed. "Perhaps you are right, I do not know. Only the Runestaff could prove you right or wrong."

Hawkmoon got up stiffly. "I have not seen Yisselda since we returned," he said.

"She went to her bed early, I think," Bowgentle told him.

Hawkmoon was disappointed. He had looked forward to her welcome. Had wanted to tell her personally of his victories. It surprised him that she had not been there to greet him.

He shrugged. "Well, I think I'll to mine," he said. "Good night, gentlemen."

They had spoken little of their triumph since returning. Now they were experiencing the reaction of their day's work, and it all seemed a trifle remote, though tomorrow, doubtless, they would celebrate.

When he reached his room it was in darkness, but Hawkmoon sensed something odd and drew his sword before fumbling his way to a table and turning up the lamp that stood there.

Someone lay on his bed, smiling at him. It was Yisselda.

"I heard of your exploits," said she, "and wanted to give you a private welcome. You are a great hero, Dorian."

Hawkmoon felt his breathing become more rapid, felt his heart begin to pound. "Oh, Yisselda . . ."

Slowly, step by step, he advanced toward the prone girl, his conscience in conflict with his desire.

"You love me, Dorian, I know," she said softly. "Do you deny it?"

He could not. He spoke thickly. "You . . . are . . . very . . . bold . . . ," he said, trying to smile.

"Aye—for you seem extraordinarily shy. I am not immodest."

"I—I am not shy, Yisselda. But no good could come of this. I am doomed—the Black Jewel . . ."

"What is the Jewel?"

Hesitantly, he told her everything, told her that he did not know how many months Count Brass's sorcerous chains could hold the life force of the Jewel, told her that when its power was released, the Lords of the Dark Empire would be able to destroy his mind.

"So you see—you must not become attached to me . . . It would be worse if you did."

"But this Malagigi—why do you not seek his aid?"

"The journey would take months. I might waste my remaining time on a fruitless quest."

"If you loved me," she said as he sat down on the bed beside her and took her hand, "you would risk that."

"Aye," he said thoughtfully. "I would. Perhaps you are right . . ."

She reached up and drew his face toward hers, kissing his lips. The gesture was artless but full of sweetness.

Now he could not restrain himself. He kissed her passionately, held her close. "I will go to Persia," he said at length, "though the way will be perilous, for once I leave the safety of Kamarg, Meliadus's forces will seek me out . . ."

"You will come back," she said with conviction. "I know you will come back. My love will draw you to me."

"And mine to you?" He stroked her face gently. "Aye—that could be so."

"Tomorrow," she said. "Leave tomorrow and waste no time. Tonight . . ."

She kissed him again, and he returned her passion fiercely.

BOOK THREE

The histories then tell how, leaving Kamarg,
Hawkmoon flew eastward on a giant scarlet bird that
bore him a thousand miles or more before it came to
the mountains bordering the lands of the Greeks
and the Bulgars . . .

—*The High History of the Runestaff*

1

OLADAHN

The flamingo was surprisingly easy to ride, as Count Brass had assured him it would be. It responded to commands in the manner of a horse, by means of the reins attached to its curved beak, and was so graceful that never once did Hawkmoon fear falling. In spite of the bird's refusal to fly when it rained, it carried him ten times more swiftly than a horse, needing to rest only for a short time at midday and sleeping, like Hawkmoon, at night.

The high, soft saddle, with its curved pommel, was comfortable, and from it hung panniers of provisions. A harness secured Hawkmoon in his saddle. Its long neck stretched straight before it and its great wings beating slowly, the scarlet bird bore him over mountains, valleys, forests, and plains. Hawkmoon always tried to let the bird come down near rivers or lakes where it could find food to its liking.

Occasionally, Hawkmoon's head would throb, reminding him of the urgency of his mission, but as his winged mount took him farther and farther eastward and the air grew steadily warmer, Hawkmoon's spirits began to rise, and it seemed that the possibilities of returning soon to Yisselda were increasing.

About a week after he had left Kamarg, he was flying over a range of craggy mountains looking for a place to land. It was late evening, and the bird was wearying, dropping lower and lower until the gloomy peaks were all around them and still no water could be seen. Then, suddenly, Hawkmoon saw the figure of a man on the rocky slopes below and, almost instantly, the flamingo screamed, flapping its wings wildly, rocking in the air. Hawkmoon saw a long arrow jutting from its side. A second arrow thudded into the bird's neck, and with a croak, it began to fall rapidly toward the ground. Hawkmoon clung to the pommel of his saddle as the air tore through his hair. He saw the rock rise up, felt a great concussion, and then his head had struck something and he seemed to tumble sickeningly into a black, bottomless well.

Hawkmoon awoke in panic. It seemed that the Black Jewel had been given its life and was even now gnawing at his brain like a rat at a grain sack. He put both hands to his head and felt cuts and bumps, realizing with relief that the pain was physical, resulting from his crash to earth. It was dark, and it seemed that he lay in a cave. Peering forward he saw a flicker of firelight beyond the cave's entrance. He got up and began to make his way toward it.

Near the opening, his foot stumbled against something and

he saw his gear piled on the floor. Everything was neatly stacked—saddle, panniers, sword, and dagger. He reached for the sword and softly withdrew it from its scabbard; then he went out.

His face was struck by the heat from the great bonfire a short distance away. Over it, a spit had been constructed, and on the spit turned the huge carcass of the flamingo, trussed, plucked, and bereft of head and claws. Turning the spit by means of a complicated arrangement of leather thongs, which he dampened from time to time, was the stocky figure of a man almost half Hawkmoon's size.

As Hawkmoon approached, the little man turned, saw the blade, yelled, and jumped away from the fire. The Duke of Köln was astonished; the creature's face was covered with fine, reddish hair and thicker fur of the same colour seemed to cover his body. He was dressed in a leather jerkin and a leather divided kilt supported by a wide belt. On his feet were boots of soft doeskin, and he wore a cap into which were stuck four or five of the finest flamingo feathers, doubtless purloined from the bird's plumage during the plucking.

He backed away from Hawkmoon, hands raised in a placatory gesture. "Forgive me, master. I am deeply regretful, I assure you. Had I but known that the bird bore a rider, I would not, of course, have shot it. But all I saw was a dinner not to be missed . . ."

Hawkmoon lowered the sword. "Who are you? Indeed—*what* are you?" He put one hand to his head. The heat from the fire and the exertion had made him dizzy.

"I am Oladahn, kin to the Mountain Giants," began the little man. "Well-known in these parts . . ."

"Giant? *Giant!*" Hawkmoon laughed hoarsely, swayed, and fell, losing consciousness again.

Next time he awoke, it was to sniff the delicious smell of roasting fowl. He savoured it before he realized what it meant. He had been propped up just within the cave entrance, and his sword had vanished. The little furry man came hesitantly forward, offering him an enormous drumstick.

"Eat, master, and you'll feel better," said Oladahn.

Hawkmoon accepted the great piece of meat. "I suppose I might as well," said he, "since you have robbed me, almost certainly, of everything I desired."

"You were fond of the bird, master?"

"No—but I am in mortal danger, and the flamingo was my only hope of escape." Hawkmoon chewed at the tough flesh.

"Someone pursues you, then?"

"Something pursues me—an unusual and disgusting doom . . ." And Hawkmoon found himself telling his tale to the creature whose action had brought that doom closer. Even as he spoke, he found it hard to understand why he confided in Oladahn. There was something so grave about his half-human face, something so attentive about the way he cocked his little head, his eyes widening at each new detail, that Hawkmoon's natural reticence was forgotten. "And now here I am," he concluded at last, "eating the bird that was to be my possible salvation."

"It is an ironic tale, my lord," Oladahn sighed, wiping grease from his whiskers, "and it clouds my heart to realize that it was my greedy stomach that brought about this last misfortune.

Tomorrow I will do what I can to rectify my mistake and find you a steed of some sort to carry you on to the East."

"Something that can fly?"

"Sadly, no. A goat's the beast I had in mind." Before Hawkmoon could speak, Oladahn continued, "I have a certain influence in these mountains, being regarded as something of a curiosity. I am a crossbred animal, you see, the result of a union between an adventurous youth of peculiar tastes—a sorcerer of sorts—and a Mountain Giantess. Alas, I am an orphan now, for Mother ate Father one hard winter, then Mother was eaten in turn by my Uncle Barkyos—the terror of these parts, largest and fiercest of the Mountain Giants. Since then, I have lived alone, with only my poor father's books for company. I am an outcast—too strange to be accepted either by my father's race or my mother's—living on my wits. If I were not so small, doubtless I should have been eaten, also, by Uncle Barkyos by now . . ."

Oladahn's face looked so comic in its melancholy that Hawkmoon could no longer bear him even a trace of malice. Besides, he was feeling tired from the heat of the fire and the large meal he had eaten. "Enough, friend Oladahn. Let us forget what cannot be rectified and sleep now. In the morning we must find a new mount for me to ride to Persia."

And they slept, to awaken at dawn to see the fire still flickering under the carcass of the bird and a group of men, in fur and iron, breakfasting off it in some glee.

"Brigands!" Oladahn cried, springing up in alarm. "I should not have left the fire!"

"Where did you hide my sword?" Hawkmoon asked him, but already two of the men, smelling strongly of ancient animal fat, had swaggered toward them, drawing crude swords. Hawkmoon rose slowly to his feet, ready to defend himself as best he could, but Oladahn was already speaking.

"I know you, Rekner," he said, pointing at the largest of the brigands. "And you should know that I am Oladahn of the Mountain Giants. Now that you have had your meal, be off, or my kin will come and slay you."

Rekner grinned, unperturbed, picking his teeth with a dirty fingernail. "I have heard of you, indeed, littlest of giants, and I see nothing to fear, though I've been told that the villagers hereabouts avoid you. But villagers are not brave brigands, eh? Hush now, or we'll kill you slowly instead of quickly."

Oladahn seemed to wilt, but he continued to stare hard at the brigand chieftain. Rekner laughed. "Now, what treasures have you got in that cave of yours?"

Oladahn was swaying from side to side, as if in terror, crooning softly to himself. Hawkmoon looked from him to the brigand and back again, wondering if he could dash into the cave and find his sword in time. Now Oladahn's crooning grew louder, and Rekner paused, the smile freezing on his face and a glassy look coming into his eyes as Oladahn peered into them. Suddenly the little man flung up a hand, pointing and speaking in a cold voice. "Sleep, Rekner!"

Rekner slumped to the ground, and his men cursed, starting forward, then stopping as Oladahn kept his hand raised. "Beware my power, scavengers, for Oladahn is the son of a sorcerer."

The brigands hesitated, glancing at their prone leader. Hawkmoon looked in astonishment at the furry creature who held the warlike men at bay, then ducked into the cave and found his sword rescabbarded. He drew the belt that held it and the dagger about his waist and buckled it, pulling forth the blade and returning to Oladahn's side. The little man muttered from the corner of his mouth, "Bring your provisions. Their steeds are tethered at the bottom of the slope. We'll use them to escape, for Rekner will waken any instant, and I cannot hold them after that."

Hawkmoon got the panniers, and he and Oladahn began to back down the slope, their feet scraping on the loose rock and scrub. Rekner was already stirring. He gave a groan and sat up. His men bent to help him to his feet. "Now," said Oladahn, and turned to run. Hawkmoon followed and there, to his surprise, were half a dozen goats the size of ponies, each animal with a sheepskin saddle. Oladahn swung himself up onto the nearest and held the bridle of another for Hawkmoon. The Duke of Köln hesitated for a moment, then smiled wryly and climbed into the saddle. Rekner and his brigands were racing down the hill toward them. With the flat of his sword, Hawkmoon slapped at the rumps of the remaining goats and they began to spring away.

"Follow me!" cried Oladahn, urging his goat down the mountain toward a narrow trail. But Rekner's men had reached Hawkmoon, and his bright sword met their dull ones as they hacked savagely at him. He stabbed one man through the heart, struck another in the side, managed to slam the side of his blade down on Rekner's pate, then was riding the leaping goat in hot pursuit of the strange little man, the brigands roaring oaths and staggering after him.

The goat moved in a series of leaps, jolting the bones of his body, but soon they had reached the trail and were riding down a tortuous path around the mountain, the cries of the brigands growing fainter and fainter. Oladahn turned with a grin of triumph. "We have our mounts, Lord Hawkmoon, eh? Easier than even I expected. A good omen! Follow me. I'll lead you to your road."

Hawkmoon smiled in spite of himself. Oladahn's company was intoxicating, and his curiosity about the little man, coupled with his growing respect and gratitude for the manner in which he had saved their lives, made Hawkmoon forget almost completely that the furry kin of the Mountain Giants had been the initial cause of his new troubles.

Oladahn insisted on riding with him for several days, all the way through the mountains, until they reached a wide yellow plain and Oladahn pointed, saying, "That is the way you must go."

"I thank you," Hawkmoon said, staring now toward Asia. "It is a shame that we must part."

"Aha!" grinned Oladahn, rubbing at the red fur on his face. "I'd agree with that sentiment. Come, I'll ride with you a way to keep you company on the plain." And with that he urged his goat forward again.

Hawkmoon laughed, shrugged, and followed.

2

THE CARAVAN OF AGONOSVOS

It began to rain almost as soon as they reached the plain, and the goats, which had borne them so well through the mountains, were unused to the yielding earth and moved slowly. For a month they traveled, hunched in their cloaks, shivering from the damp that chilled them to their vitals, and Hawkmoon's head throbbed often. When the throbbing came, he would not speak to the solicitous Oladahn but would bury his head in his arms, his face pale and his teeth clenched, tormented eyes staring at nothing. He knew that at Castle Brass the sentience of the Jewel was beginning to break the bonds the count had wrought, and he despaired of seeing Yisselda again.

Rain beat down, and a cold wind blustered, and through the sweeping curtain of water Hawkmoon saw vast stretches of fenland ahead of them, broken by clumps of gorse and black, shrunken trees. He had little idea of his bearings, for most of the time clouds obscured the sky. The only rough indication of direction was in the manner in which the shrubs grew in this part of the world, leaning almost invariably toward the south. He had not expected to meet such country so far to the east, and he gathered that its characteristics were the result of some event that had taken place during the Tragic Millennium.

Hawkmoon brushed his damp hair from his eyes, feeling the hard touch of the Black Jewel embedded in his forehead. He shivered, glancing at Oladahn's miserable face, then back through the rain. There was a dark outline in the distance that might indicate a forest where they would at least have some protection from the rain. The pointed hoofs of the goats stumbled through the swampy grass. Hawkmoon's head began to tingle, and again he felt the gnawing sensation in his brain and a nausea in his chest. He gasped, pressing one forearm against his skull while Oladahn looked on in mute sympathy.

At length they reached the low-lying trees. They found the going even slower than it had been and avoided the ponds of dark water that had formed everywhere. The trunks and branches of the trees seemed malformed, twisting toward the ground rather than away from it. The bark was black or dark brown, and at this season there was no foliage. In spite of this, the forest seemed thick and hard to penetrate. At its edge water glinted, a shallow moat protecting the trees.

Their mounts' hoofs splashed through the muddy water as they entered the forest, bending low to avoid the curling branches. Even here the ground was swampy, and pools had formed at the bases of the trunks, but there was little shelter, after all, from the perpetually falling rain.

They camped that evening on relatively dry ground, and although Hawkmoon made some attempt to help Oladahn build a fire, he was soon forced to lie with his back against a tree trunk, panting and clutching his head while the little man finished the work.

The next morning they moved on through the forest, Oladahn leading Hawkmoon's mount, for the Duke of Köln was now slumped across its neck. Toward the latter part of the morning they heard human voices and turned their beasts toward the sound.

It was a caravan of sorts, labouring through the mud and water between the trees. Some fifteen wagons, with rain-soaked silk canopies of scarlet, yellow, blue, and green. Mules and oxen strained to haul them, and their feet slipped in mud, and their muscles bulged and rippled as they were goaded on by their drivers, who stood beside them with whips and spiked sticks. At the wheels of the wagons other men sweated to help turn them, and at the backs of the wagons leaned more who pushed with all their might. Yet in spite of this great effort, the wagons hardly moved.

It was not so much this sight that made the two travelers wonder, but the nature of the people of the caravan. Through his clouded eyes, Hawkmoon saw them and wondered.

Without exception they were grotesque. Dwarves and midgets, giants and fat men, men with fur growing all over them (rather like Oladahn, save that the fur of these was unpleasant to look upon), others pale and hairless, one man with three arms, another with one; two cloven-footed people—a man and a woman—children with beards, hermaphrodites with the organs of both sexes, others with mottled skins like snakes, and others with tails, misshapen limbs and warped bodies; faces with features missing or else abnormally proportioned; some hunchbacked, some without necks, some with foreshortened arms and legs, one with purple hair and a horn growing from his forehead. And only in their eyes was there any similarity, for every expression was one of dull despair as the bizarre band toiled to move the caravan a few feet through the wooded marsh.

It seemed that they were in hell and looked upon the damned.

The forest smell of damp bark and wet mould was now mingled with other scents, harder to identify. There was the stink of men and beasts, of heavy perfume and rich spices, but besides these there was something else that lay over them all and made Oladahn shudder. Hawkmoon had raised himself up from his mount's neck and sniffed the air like a wary wolf. He glanced at Oladahn, frowning. The deformed creatures did not seem to notice the newcomers but continued to work in silence. There was only the sound of the wagons creaking and the animals snorting and splashing in their yokes.

Oladahn tugged at his reins, as if to pass the caravan by, but Hawkmoon did not follow his example. He continued to stare thoughtfully at the weird procession.

"Come," said Oladahn. "There is danger here, Lord Hawkmoon."

"We must get our bearings—find out where we are and how

far we must travel over this plain," Hawkmoon said in a harsh whisper. "Besides, our provisions are almost gone . . ."

"We might come upon some game in the forest."

Hawkmoon shook his head. "No. Also I think I know to whom this caravan belongs."

"Who?"

"A man I have heard of but never encountered. A countryman of mine—a kinsman even—who left Köln some nine centuries ago."

"Nine centuries? Impossible!"

"Not so. Lord Agonosvos is immortal—or nearly. If it be he, then he could help us, for I am still his rightful ruler . . ."

"He would have loyalty to Köln, after nine hundred years?"

"Let us see." Hawkmoon urged his beast toward the head of the caravan, where a tall wagon swayed, its canopy of golden silk, its carriage carved in complicated patterns, painted in bright primaries. Ill at ease, Oladahn followed less rapidly. In the front of the wagon, seated well back to avoid the greater part of the drifting rain, was a figure huddled in a rich bearskin cloak, a plain black helm covering its whole face save for the eyes. It moved as it saw Dorian Hawkmoon regarding it and a thin, hollow sound came from the helm.

"Lord Agonosvos," Hawkmoon said. "I am the Duke von Köln, last of the line begun a thousand years since."

The figure answered in a low, laconic tone. "A Hawkmoon, I can see that. Landless now, eh? Granbretan took Köln, did it not?"

"Aye . . ."

"And so we are both banished; myself by your ancestor, and you by the conqueror."

"Be that as it may, I am still the last of my line and thus your master." Hawkmoon's tormented face stared hard at the figure.

"Master, is it? Authority over me was renounced when I was sent to the wild lands by Duke Dietrich."

"Not so, as you well know. No man of Köln can ever refuse his prince's will."

"Can he not?" Agonosvos laughed quietly. "Can he not?"

Hawkmoon made to turn away, but Agonosvos raised a thin, slim-fingered hand that was bone-white. "Stay. I have offended you and must make amends. How can I serve you?"

"You admit your loyalty to me?"

"I admit to impoliteness. You seem weary. I will stop my caravan and entertain you. What of your servant?"

"He is not my servant but my friend. Oladahn of the Bulgar Mountains."

"A friend? And not of your race? Still, let him join us." Agonosvos leaned from his wagon to call languidly to his men to stop their labours. Instantly, they relaxed, standing where they were, their bodies limp and their eyes still full of dumb despair.

"What do you think of my collection?" Agonosvos asked when they had dismounted and climbed into the gloom of the wagon's interior. "Such curiosities once amused me, but now I find them dull and they must work to justify their existence. I have one at least of almost every type." He glanced at Oladahn. "Including yours. Some I crossbred myself."

Oladahn shifted his position uncomfortably. It was unnaturally warm within the confines of the wagon; yet there was no sign of a stove or any other heating apparatus. Agonosvos poured them wine from a blue gourd. The wine, too, was a deep, lustrous blue.

The ancient exile of Köln still wore his black, featureless helm, and his black, sardonic eyes looked at Hawkmoon a trifle calculatingly.

Hawkmoon was making a great effort to appear in good health, but it was plain that Agonosvos guessed the truth when he handed him a golden goblet of wine and said, "This will make you feel better, my lord."

The wine did, in fact, revive him, and soon the pain had gone again. Agonosvos asked him how he had come to be in these parts, and Hawkmoon told him a considerable part of his tale. "So," said Agonosvos, "you want my help, eh? For the sake of our ancient kinship, hmm? Well, I will brood upon that. In the meantime I will set a wagon aside so that you may rest. We will discuss the matter further in the morning."

Hawkmoon and Oladahn did not sleep immediately. They sat up in the silks and furs Agonosvos had lent them and discussed the strange sorcerer. "He reminds me uncommon much of those Dark Empire Lords you told me of," Oladahn said. "I think he means us ill. Perhaps he wishes to be avenged on you for the wrong he thinks your forefather did him—perhaps he wants to add me to his collection." He shuddered.

"Aye," Hawkmoon said thoughtfully. "But it would be unwise to anger him without reason. He could be useful to us. We'll sleep on it."

"Sleep warily," Oladahn cautioned.

But Hawkmoon slept deeply and awakened to find himself bound in tight leather thongs that had been wrapped round and round his body and then tugged to secure him. He struggled, glaring up at the enigmatic helm that covered the face of his immortal kinsman. There came a soft chuckle from Agonosvos.

"You knew of me, last of the Hawkmoons—but you did not know as much as you should. Know you not that many of my years were spent in Londra, teaching the Lords of Granbretan my secrets? We have long had an alliance, the Dark Empire and I. Baron Meliadus spoke of you when last I saw him. He will pay me anything I desire for your living body."

"Where is my companion?"

"The furry creature? Scampered into the night when he heard our approach. They are all the same, these beast folk—timid and faint-hearted friends."

"So you intend to deliver me to Baron Meliadus?"

"You heard me perfectly. Aye, that is just what I intend. I'll leave this clumsy caravan to wend its way as best it can till I return. We'll move on swifter steeds—special steeds I have kept for such a time as this. I have already sent a messenger ahead of me to tell the baron of my catch. You—bear him forth!"

At Agonosvos's command, two midgets hurried forward to pick Hawkmoon up in their long, well-muscled arms and clamber out of the wagon with him into the grey light of early dawn.

A drizzle still fell, and through it Hawkmoon saw two great horses, both with coats of lustrous blue, intelligent eyes, and powerful limbs. He had never seen such fine beasts. "I bred them myself," Agonosvos said, "not for strangeness, in this case, but for speed. We shall soon be in Londra, you and I." He chuckled again as Hawkmoon was slung over the back of one of the steeds and roped to the stirrups.

He climbed into the saddle of the second horse, took the bridle of Hawkmoon's, and spurred forward. Hawkmoon was alarmed at the swift movement of the horse. It moved easily, galloping almost as fast as his flamingo had flown. But where the bird had borne him toward salvation, this horse took him closer to his doom. In an agony of mind, Hawkmoon decided that his lot was hopeless.

They galloped for a long time through the slushy earth of the forest. Hawkmoon's face became coated with mud, and he could see only by blinking heavily and craning his neck up.

Then, much later, he heard Agonosvos curse and shout. "Out of my way—out of my way!" Hawkmoon tried to peer forward but could see nothing save the hindquarters of Agonosvos's horse and a little of the man's cloak. Dimly, he heard another voice but could not distinguish what it said.

"Aaah! May Kaldereen eat your eyes!" Agonosvos now seemed to be reeling in his saddle. The two horses slowed their pace, then halted. Hawkmoon saw Agonosvos sway forward and then fall into the mud, crawling through it and trying to rise. There was an arrow in his side. Helpless, Hawkmoon wondered what new danger had arisen. Was he to be killed here rather than at the Court of King Huon?

A small figure came into view, skipping over the struggling body of Agonosvos and slashing at Hawkmoon's bonds. Hawkmoon dropped from the saddle, holding on to the pommel and rubbing at his numbed arms and legs. Oladahn grinned at him. "You'll find your sword in the sorcerer's baggage," he said.

Hawkmoon grinned in relief. "I thought you'd fled back to your mountains."

Oladahn began to reply, but Hawkmoon gasped a warning. "Agonosvos!" The sorcerer had risen to his feet, clutching at the arrow in his side and staggering toward the little mountain man. Hawkmoon forgot his own pain, ran to the sorcerer's horse, and tore at the man's rolled goods until he found his sword. Oladahn was now wrestling in the mud with Agonosvos.

Hawkmoon sprang at them but dared not risk stabbing at the sorcerer lest he harm his friend. He leaned down and hauled on Agonosvos's shoulder, dragging the enraged man backward. He heard a snarl issue from the helm, and Agonosvos drew his own sword from its scabbard. It whistled through the air as he struck at Hawkmoon. Hawkmoon, still hardly able to stand, met the blow and staggered backward. The sorcerer struck again.

Hawkmoon deflected the blade, swung his sword somewhat weakly at Agonosvos's head, missed, and was just in time to parry the next stroke. Then he saw an opening and drove the blade point-first into the sorcerer's belly. The man shrieked and backed away, curiously stiff-legged, his hands clutching Hawkmoon's sword, which had been wrenched from the Duke of Köln's hands. Then he spread his arms wide, began to speak, and fell sprawling into the dark water of a shallow pool.

Panting, Hawkmoon leaned against the bole of a tree, the pain in his limbs increasing as the circulation returned.

Oladahn rose from the mud, hardly recognizable. A quiver of arrows had been torn loose from his belt, and he picked it up now, inspecting the fletchings. "Some are ruined, but I'll soon replace 'em," he said.

"Where did you get them?"

"Last night, I decided to make my own inspection of

Agonosvos's camp. I found the bow and arrows in one of the wagons and thought they might be useful. Returning, I saw Agonosvos enter our wagon and guessed his business, so I remained hidden and followed you."

"But how could you follow such fast horses?" Hawkmoon asked.

"I found an even faster ally," Oladahn grinned, and pointed through the trees. Coming toward them was a grotesque creature with incredibly long legs, the rest of his body of normal size. "This is Vlespeen. He hates Agonosvos and willingly aided me."

Vlespeen peered down at them. "You killed him," he said. "Good."

Oladahn inspected Agonosvos's baggage. He brandished a roll of parchment. "A map. And enough provisions to get us all to the coast." He unrolled the map. "It's not far. Look."

They gathered around the map, and Hawkmoon saw that it was scarcely more than a hundred miles to the Mermian Sea. Vlespeen wandered away to where Agonosvos had fallen; perhaps to gloat over the corpse. A moment later they heard him scream and turned to see the body of the sorcerer, brandishing the sword that had slain him, walking stiffly toward the long-legged man. The sword ripped upward into Vlespeen's stomach, and his legs collapsed under him, jerked like a puppet's, and then were still. Hawkmoon was horrified. From within the helm came a dry chuckle. "Fools! I have lived for nine hundred years. In that time I have learned how to cheat all forms of death."

Without thinking, Hawkmoon leaped at him, knowing it was his one chance to save his life. Even though he had survived a blow that should have been mortal, Agonosvos had evidently been weakened. The two struggled on the edge of the pool, while Oladahn danced around them, jumping at last upon the sorcerer's back and wrenching the tight helm from his head. Agonosvos howled, and Hawkmoon felt nausea overcome him as he stared at the white, fleshless head that was revealed. It was the face of an ancient corpse; a corpse that the worms had chewed upon. Agonosvos covered the face in his hands and staggered away.

As Hawkmoon picked up his sword and made to mount the great blue horse, he heard a voice come calling to him through the woods.

"I shall not forget this, Dorian Hawkmoon. You'll yet make sport for Baron Meliadus—and I shall be there to watch!"

Hawkmoon shuddered and urged the horse southward, where the map had shown the Mermian Sea to lie. Oladahn followed.

Within two days the sky had lightened and a yellow sun shone in blue, and ahead of them was a town beside the glinting sea, where they might take ship for Turkia.

3

THE WARRIOR IN JET
AND GOLD

The heavy Turkian merchantman clove through the calm waters of the ocean, foam breaking over its bow, its single lateen sail stretched like a bird's wing as it took the strong wind. The captain of the vessel, in golden tasseled hat and braided jacket, his long skirts held to his ankles by bands of gold, stood with Hawkmoon and Oladahn in the stern of the ship. The captain jerked his thumb at the two huge blue horses corralled on the lower deck. "Fine beasts, masters. I've never seen the like in these parts." He scratched at his pointed beard. "You would not sell them? I'm part owner of this vessel and could afford a good price."

Hawkmoon shook his head. "Those horses are worth more to me than any riches."

"I can believe it," replied the captain, missing his meaning. He looked up as the man in the topmast yelled and waved, stretching his arm to the west.

Hawkmoon glanced in the same direction and saw three small sails rising over the horizon. The captain raised his spyglass. "By Rakar—Dark Empire ships!" He passed the glass to Hawkmoon. Hawkmoon saw the black sails of the vessels clearly now. Each was emblazoned with the shark symbol of the Empire's warfleet.

"Do they mean us harm?" he asked.

"They mean harm to all not of their own kind," the captain said grimly. "We can only pray they haven't seen us. The sea's becoming thick with their craft. A year ago . . ." He paused to yell orders to his men. The ship jumped as staysails were added forard. "A year ago there were few of them, and trading peacefully for the most part. Now they dominate the seas. You'll find their armies in Turkia, Syria, Persia—everywhere—spreading insurrection, aiding local revolts. My guess is they'll have the East under their heel as they have the West—give 'em a couple of years."

Soon the Dark Empire ships were below the horizon again, and the captain breathed a sigh of relief. "I'll not be comfortable," said he, "till port's in sight."

The Turkian port was seen at sunset, and they were forced to lie offshore until morning, when they sailed in on the tide and docked.

Not much later, the three Dark Empire warships came into the harbour, and Hawkmoon and Oladahn deemed it expedient to purchase what provisions they could and follow the map eastward, for Persia.

A week later, the great horses had borne them well past Ankara and across the Kizilirmac River, and they were riding through hill country where all seemed turned to yellow and brown by the burning sun. On several occasions they had seen armies pass by but had avoided them. The armies consisted of local troops, often augmented by masked warriors of Granbretan. Hawkmoon was disturbed by this, for he had not expected the Dark Empire's influence to stretch this far. Once, they witnessed a battle from a distance, seeing the disciplined forces of Granbretan easily defeat the opposing army. Now Hawkmoon rode desperately toward Persia.

A month later, as their horses trotted along the shores of a vast lake, Oladahn and Hawkmoon were suddenly surprised by a force of some twenty warriors who appeared over the crest of a hill and came charging toward them. The warriors' masks flashed in the sun, adding to their fierce appearance—the masks of the Order of the Wolf.

"Ho! The two our master seeks!" cried one of the leading horsemen. "The reward is large for the tall one if taken alive."

Oladahn said calmly, "I fear, Lord Dorian, that we're doomed."

"Make them kill you," said Hawkmoon grimly, and drew his sword. If the horses had not been weary, he would have fled the warriors, but he knew that that would be useless now.

Soon the wolf-masked riders were all around them. Hawkmoon had the slight advantage of wishing to kill them, while they wanted him alive. He struck one full in the mask with the pommel of his sword, sheered half-through another's arm, stabbed a third in the groin, and knocked a fourth from his horse. Now they were in the shallows of the lake, the steeds' hoofs splashing in the water. Hawkmoon saw Oladahn accounting well for himself, but then the furry little man gave a cry and fell from his saddle. Hawkmoon could not see him for the press, but he cursed and struck about him with a greater will.

Now they closed in so that he hardly had room to swing his sword. He realized, sickeningly, they would take him in a few moments. He struggled and smote on, his ears full of the clang of metal, his nostrils clogged with the smell of blood.

Then he felt the pressure give way and saw through a forest of swords that an ally had joined him. He had seen the figure before—but only in dreams, or visions very similar to dreams. It was the one he had seen in France and later in Kamarg. He was dressed in full armour of jet and gold, a long helm completely enclosing his face. He swung a six-foot broadsword and rode a white battle charger as big as Hawkmoon's. Wherever he struck, men fell, and soon there were only a few wolf warriors still horsed and these at length galloped off through the water, leaving their dead and wounded behind.

Hawkmoon saw one of the fallen riders struggle up. Then he saw another rise beside him and realized it was Oladahn. The little man still had his sword and was defending himself desperately against the Granbretanian. Hawkmoon pushed his horse through the shallows and brought his sword round in a great swing to strike the wolf warrior in the back, shearing through his mail and leather undershirt and cutting deep into his flesh.

With a groan the man fell, and his blood joined that already reddening the waters.

Hawkmoon turned to where the Warrior in Jet and Gold sat his horse silently.

"I thank you, my lord," he said. "You have followed me a long way." He resheathed his sword.

"Longer than you know, Dorian Hawkmoon," came the rich, echoing voice of the warrior. "You ride to Hamadan?"

"Aye—to seek the sorcerer Malagigi."

"Good. I will ride with you some of the way. It is not far now."

"Who are you?" Hawkmoon asked. "Who may I thank?"

"I am the Warrior in Jet and Gold. Do not thank me for saving your life. You do not realize yet what I have saved it for. Come." And the warrior led them away from the lake.

A little later, as they rested and ate, the warrior, with one leg crooked beneath him, sat some distance off. Hawkmoon asked him, "Know you much of Malagigi? Will he help me?"

"I know him," said the Warrior in Jet and Gold. "Perhaps he will help you. But know you this—there is civil war in Hamadan. Queen Frawbra's brother, Nahak, schemes against her, and he is aided by many who wear the masks of those we fought at the lake."

4

MALAGIGI

A week later they looked down on the city of Hamadan, all white and gleaming in the bright sun, with its spires, domes, and minarets chased with gold, silver, and mother-of-pearl.

"I will leave you now," said the mysterious warrior, turning his horse. "Farewell, Dorian Hawkmoon. Doubtless we shall meet again."

Hawkmoon watched him ride away through the hills; then he and Oladahn urged their horses toward the city.

But as they approached the gates they heard a great noise from behind the walls. It was the sound of fighting, the shouts of warriors and the screams of beasts, and suddenly, out of the gates burst a great rabble of soldiers, many of them badly wounded and all much battered. The two men pulled their horses up short but were soon surrounded by the fleeing army. A group of riders charged past them, and Hawkmoon heard one cry—"All is lost! Nahak wins the day!"

Following them came a huge bronze war chariot pulled by four black horses, and in it was a raven-haired woman in blue plate armour who shouted at her men, urging them to turn and fight. The woman was young and very beautiful, with huge, dark, slanting eyes that blazed with anger and frustration. In one hand she held a scimitar, which she brandished high.

She dragged at the reins as she saw the bewildered Hawkmoon and Oladahn. "Who are you? More Dark Empire mercenaries?"

"No—I am an enemy of the Dark Empire," Hawkmoon said. "What is happening?"

"An uprising. My brother, Nahak, and his allies broke through the secret passageways that lead from the desert and surprised us. If you are Granbretan's enemy, then you had best flee now! They have battle beasts with them that . . ." Then she was yelling again at her men and had moved on.

"We had best return to the hills," Oladahn murmured, but Hawkmoon shook his head.

"I must find Malagigi. He is somewhere in this city. There is little time left."

They pushed their horses through the throng and into the city. Up ahead some men were still fighting in the streets, and the spiked helmets of the local soldiers mingled with the wolf helms of the Dark Empire warriors. Everywhere was carnage. Hawkmoon and Oladahn galloped up a side street where there was little fighting at present and emerged into an open square. On the opposite side they saw gigantic winged beasts, like great black bats but with long arms and curved claws. They were rending at

the retreating warriors, and some were already feasting on the corpses. Here and there Nahak's men were trying to urge these battle beasts on, but it was plain the giant bats had already served their purpose.

A bat turned and saw them. Hawkmoon yelled to Oladahn to follow him down a narrow lane, but the bat was already pursuing them, half-running, half-flapping through the air, a disgusting whistling sound coming from its jaws, a dreadful stench exuding from its body. Into the lane they rode, but the bat squeezed between the houses and continued to follow them. Then, from the opposite end of the street, came some half a dozen wolf-masked riders. Hawkmoon drew his sword and charged on. There was little else to do.

He met the first of the riders with a lunge that ripped the man from his saddle. A sword slashed at his shoulder, and he felt it bite home, but he continued to fight in spite of the pain. The battle beast screamed, and the wolf warriors began to back their horses away in panic.

Hawkmoon and Oladahn burst through them and found themselves in a larger square that was empty of the living. Only corpses lay everywhere on cobblestones and pavements. Hawkmoon saw a yellow-robed man dart from a doorway to bend beside a corpse and cut at the purse and jeweled dagger in its belt. The man looked up in panic and tried to dash back into his house when he saw the Duke of Köln, but Oladahn blocked his way. Hawkmoon pressed his sword into the man's cheek. "Which way to Malagigi's house?"

The man pointed a trembling finger and croaked, "That way, masters. The one with the dome that has zodiacal signs inlaid in ebony on a silver roof. Down that street. Do not kill me. I . . ." He sighed in relief as Hawkmoon turned his great blue horse and rode for the street he had indicated.

The domed house with the zodiacal signs was soon in sight. Hawkmoon stopped at the gate and hammered on it with the pommel of his sword. His head was beginning to throb again, and he knew instinctively that Count Brass's spells could not hold the Black Jewel's life for much longer. He realized that he should have approached the sorcerer's house in a more courteous manner, but there was no time, with Granbretan's soldiers everywhere in the streets of the city. Overhead two of the giant bats flapped, seeking victims.

At last the gate swung open and four huge Negroes armed with pikes and dressed in purple robes barred the way. Hawkmoon saw a courtyard beyond them. He tried to ride forward, but the pikes menaced him immediately. "What business have you with our master, Malagigi?" one of the Negroes asked.

"I seek his help. It is a matter of great importance. I am in peril."

A figure appeared on the steps leading to the house. The man was clad in a simple white toga. He had long grey hair and was clean-shaven. His face was lined and old, but the skin had a youthful appearance.

"Why should Malagigi help you?" the man asked. "You are from the West, I see. The people of the West bring war and dissension to Hamadan. Begone! I'll have none of you!"

"You are the Lord Malagigi?" Hawkmoon began. "I am a victim of these same people. Help me and I can help you be rid of them. Please, I beg you—"

"Begone. I'll play no part in your .internal warring!" The
Negroes pressed the two men back, and the gates closed.

Hawkmoon began to bang again on the gates, but then Oladahn
gripped his arm and pointed. Up the street toward them came
some six wolf-helmed riders led by one whose ornate mask Hawkmoon instantly recognized. It was Meliadus.

"Ha! Your time is near, Hawkmoon!" screamed Meliadus in
triumph, drawing his sword and charging forward.

Hawkmoon wrenched his horse about. Although his hatred for
Meliadus burned as deeply as ever, he knew he could not fight at
that moment. He and Oladahn fled back down the street, their
powerful horses outdistancing those of Meliadus's men.

Agonosvos or his messenger must have told Meliadus where
Hawkmoon was bound, and the baron must have come here to join
his own men, help them take Hamadan, and wreak his personal
vengeance on Hawkmoon.

Down one narrow street after another Hawkmoon dashed, until he had for the moment lost his pursuer. "We must escape the
city," he shouted to Oladahn. "It is our only chance. Perhaps later
we can sneak back and convince Malagigi to help us . . ." His
voice trailed off as one of the gigantic bats swooped suddenly
down, to alight immediately in front of them and begin to stalk
forward, claws outstretched. Beyond this creature was an open
gate and freedom.

So full of desperation was Hawkmoon now, since Malagigi
had refused him, that he charged straight at the battle beast, sword
slashing at its cruel claws, flinging himself against it. The bat
whistled, and the claws struck, clutching Hawkmoon by his already wounded arm. The young nobleman brought his sword up

again and again, hewing at the thing's wrist until black blood spurted and the tendon was severed. The beaked mouth clicked open and thrust at Hawkmoon. The horse reared as the head came down, and Hawkmoon thrust his sword up wildly, striking for the huge, beady eye. The sword plunged in. The creature screamed. Yellow mucus began to pour from the wound.

Hawkmoon struck a second time. The thing reeled and began to fall toward him. Hawkmoon managed to pull his horse aside barely in time as the battle beast collapsed. Now he raced for the gate and the hills beyond, Oladahn in his wake calling, "You have killed it, Lord Dorian! This is the stuff of the lays!" And the little man laughed with a fierce joy.

Soon they were in the hills, joining the hundreds of beaten warriors who had survived the battle in the city. They rode slowly now and at length came to a shallow valley where they saw the bronze chariot that the warrior queen had driven earlier and rank after rank of weary soldiery lying down in the tough grass while the raven-haired woman went among them. Near the chariot Hawkmoon saw another figure. It was the Warrior in Jet and Gold, and he seemed to be waiting for Hawkmoon.

Hawkmoon dismounted as he reached the warrior. The woman approached and stood leaning against her chariot, her eyes still glowing with the anger Hawkmoon had noted before.

The Warrior in Jet and Gold's rich voice came from his helmet, faintly laconic. "So Malagigi would not help you, eh?"

Hawkmoon shook his head, looking at the woman without curiosity. Disappointment filled him but was beginning to be replaced with the wild fatalism that had saved his life in his battle with the giant bat. "I am finished now," he said. "But at least I can return and find a way to destroy Meliadus."

"We have that ambition in common," said the woman. "I am Queen Frawbra. My treacherous brother covets the throne and seeks to get it with the aid of your Meliadus and his warriors. Mayhap he already has it. I cannot tell yet—but it would seem we are badly outnumbered, and there's scant chance of retaking the city."

Hawkmoon looked at her thoughtfully. "If there was a slim chance, would you seize it?"

"If there was no chance at all I'd have half a mind to try," the woman replied. "But I'm not sure my warriors would follow me!"

At that moment three more horsemen rode into the camp. Queen Frawbra called to them. "Have you just escaped the city?"

"Aye," one answered. "They are already looting. I have never seen such savage conquerors as those Westerners. Their leader— the big man—has even broken into Malagigi's house and made him prisoner!"

"What!" Hawkmoon cried. "Meliadus has the sorcerer prisoner? Ah, then, there is no hope at all for me."

The Warrior in Jet and Gold said, "Nonsense. There is still hope. So long as Meliadus keeps Malagigi alive—and one might expect him to, since the sorcerer has many secrets Meliadus desires to learn—then you have a chance. You must return to Hamadan with Queen Frawbra's armies, retake the city, and rescue Malagigi."

Hawkmoon shrugged. "But is there time? Already the Jewel shows signs of warmth. That means its life is returning. Soon I will be a mindless creature . . ."

"Then you have nothing to lose, Lord Dorian," Oladahn put

in. He laid a furry hand on Hawkmoon's arm and gave it a friendly squeeze. "Nothing to lose at all."

Hawkmoon laughed bitterly, shrugging off his friend's hand. "Aye, you're right. Nothing. Well, Queen Frawbra, what say you?"

The armoured woman said, "Let us speak to what remains of my force."

A little later, Hawkmoon stood in the chariot and addressed the battle-weary warriors. "Men of Hamadan, I have traveled for many hundreds of miles from the West, where Granbretan holds sway. My own father was tortured to death by the same Baron Meliadus who aids your queen's enemies today. I have seen whole nations reduced to ashes, their populations slain or enslaved. I have seen children crucified and hanging on gibbets. I have seen brave warriors turned to cringing dogs.

"I know that you must feel it is hopeless to resist the masked men of the Dark Empire, but they can be beaten. I, myself, was one of the commanders of an army little more than a thousand strong that put an army of Granbretan more than twenty times its number to flight. It was our will to live that enabled us to do it—our knowledge that even if we fled we should be hunted down and die eventually, ignobly.

"You can at least die courageously like men—and know that there is a chance of defeating the forces that have taken your city today . . ."

He spoke on in this vein, and gradually the tired warriors rallied. Some cheered him. Then Queen Frawbra joined him in the chariot and cried to her men to follow Hawkmoon back to

Hamadan, to strike while the enemy was unwary, while its soldiers were drunk and squabbled over their loot.

Hawkmoon's words had given them cheer; now they saw the logic of Queen Frawbra's words. They began to buckle on their weapons, adjust their armour, look for their horses.

"We'll attack tonight," the queen shouted, "giving them no time to get wind of our plan."

"I'll ride with you, I think," said the Warrior in Jet and Gold. And that night they rode to Hamadan, where the conquering soldiers reveled and the gates still stood open and hardly guarded and the battle beasts slept soundly, their stomachs full of their prey.

5

THE BLACK JEWEL'S LIFE

They had thundered into the city and were striking about them almost before the enemy realized what was happening. Hawkmoon led them. Hawkmoon's head was full of agony, and the Black Jewel had begun to pulse in his skull. His face was taut and white, and there was something about his presence that made soldiers flee before him as his horse reared and he raised his sword and screamed, "Hawkmoon! Hawkmoon!" cutting about him in a hysteria of killing.

Close behind him came the Warrior in Jet and Gold, fighting methodically with an air of detached ease. Queen Frawbra was there, driving her chariot into startled groups of warriors, and Oladahn of the Mountains stood up in his stirrups and shot arrow after arrow into the enemy.

Street by street they drove Nahak's forces and the wolf-helmed mercenaries through the city. Then Hawkmoon saw the dome of Malagigi's house and leaped his horse over the heads of those who blocked his way, reaching the house and standing upon his mount's back to grasp the top of the wall and haul himself over.

He dropped into the courtyard, just missing the sprawled body of one of Malagigi's Negro guards. The door of the house had been broken down, and the interior had been wrecked.

Stumbling through the smashed furniture, Hawkmoon found a narrow stairway. Doubtless this led to the sorcerer's laboratories. He was halfway up the stairs when a door opened at the top and two wolf-masked guards appeared, running down to meet him, their swords ready. Hawkmoon brought up his own sword to defend himself. His face was set in a death's-head grin as he fought, and his eyes blazed with a madness that was mixed fury and despair. Once, twice, his sword darted forward, and then there were two corpses tumbling down the stairs and Hawkmoon had entered the room at the top, to discover Malagigi strapped to a wall, the marks of torture on his limbs.

Quickly he cut the old man down and lowered him gently to a couch in the corner. There were benches everywhere, with alchemical apparatus and small machines resting on them. Malagigi stirred and opened his eyes.

"You must help me, sir," Hawkmoon said thickly. "I came here to save your life. At least you could try to save mine."

Malagigi raised himself on the couch, wincing in pain. "I told you—I'll do nothing for either side. Torture me if you will, as your countrymen did, but I'll not—"

"Damn you!" Hawkmoon swore. "My head's afire. I'll be lucky if I last till dawn. You must not refuse. I have come two thousand miles to seek your aid. I am as much a victim of Granbretan as you. More. I—"

"Prove that, and perhaps I'll help you," Malagigi said. "Drive the invaders from the city and then return."

"By then it will be too late. The Jewel has its life. At any moment—"

"Prove it," said Malagigi, and sank back on the couch.

Hawkmoon half-raised his sword. In his wild rage and desperation he was ready to strike the old man. But then he turned and ran back down the stairs and out into the courtyard, unbarring the gate and leaping into the saddle of his horse again.

At length he found Oladahn. "How does the battle go?" he yelled over the heads of fighting swordsmen.

"Not too well, I think. Meliadus and Nahak have regrouped and hold a good half of the city. Their main force is in the central square, where the palace stands. Queen Frawbra and your armoured friend are already leading an attack there, but I fear it's hopeless."

"Let's see for ourselves," Hawkmoon said, yanking at his mount's bridle and forcing his way through the embattled warriors, striking here and there at friend or foe, depending on which stood in his path.

Oladahn followed, and they came eventually into the great central square, to find the armies drawn up facing each other. Horsed at the head of their men were Meliadus and the rather foolish-faced Nahak, who was plainly a tool of the Dark Empire baron. Opposite them were Queen Frawbra in her battered war chariot and the Warrior in Jet and Gold.

As Hawkmoon and Oladahn entered the square, they heard

Meliadus call through the flickering torchlight that illuminated the armies, "Where is that treacherous coward Hawkmoon? Skulking in hiding, perhaps?"

Hawkmoon broke through the line of warriors, noticing that their ranks were thin. "Here I am, Meliadus. I have come to destroy you!"

Meliadus laughed. "Destroy me? Know you not that you live only by my whim? Do you feel the Black Jewel, Hawkmoon, ready to nibble at your mind?"

Involuntarily, Hawkmoon put his hand to his throbbing forehead, feeling the evil warmth of the Black Jewel, knowing that Meliadus spoke the truth. "Then why do you wait?" he said grimly.

"Because I am ready to offer you a bargain. Tell these fools their cause is hopeless. Tell them to throw down their arms—and I will spare you the worst."

Now Hawkmoon fully realized that he did, indeed, retain his mind only at the pleasure of his enemies. Meliadus had restrained his desire for immediate vengeance in the hope of forcing Hawkmoon to save Granbretan further losses.

Hawkmoon paused, unable to answer, trying to debate the issues. There was silence from his own ranks as they waited tensely to hear his decision. He knew that the whole fate of Hamadan might now depend on him. As he sat there, his mind in confusion, Oladahn nudged his arm and murmured, "Lord Dorian, take this." Hawkmoon glanced down at the thing the mountain man offered him. It was a helmet. At first he did not recognize it. Then he saw that it was the helm that had been wrenched from the skull of Agonosvos. He remembered the disgusting head that had once reposed in it and shuddered.

"Why? The thing is befouled."

"My father was a sorcerer," Oladahn reminded him. "He taught me secrets. This helm has certain properties. There are circuits built into it which will protect you for a short time from the full force of the Black Jewel's power. Put it on, my lord, I beg you."

"How can I be sure . . . ?"

"Put it on—and find out."

Gingerly Hawkmoon removed his own helmet and donned the sorcerer's. It was a tight fit and he felt stifled by it, but he realized that the Jewel no longer pulsed so fast. He smiled, and a wild feeling of elation filled him. He drew his sword. "This is my answer, Baron Meliadus!" he yelled, and charged full at the startled Lord of Granbretan.

Meliadus cursed and struggled to get his own sword from its scabbard. He had scarcely done so before Hawkmoon's sword had knocked his wolf helm clean from his head and his scowling, bewildered face was revealed. Behind Hawkmoon came the cheering soldiers of Hamadan, led by Oladahn, Queen Frawbra, and the Warrior in Jet and Gold. They clashed with the enemy, forcing them back to the gates of the palace.

From the corner of his eye, Hawkmoon saw Queen Frawbra lean from her chariot and encircle her brother's throat with her arm, dragging him from his saddle. Her hand rose and fell twice, bearing a bloody dagger, and Nahak's corpse dropped to the ground, to be trampled by the horsemen who followed the queen.

Hawkmoon was still driven by wild despair, knowing that the helm of Agonosvos could not protect him for long. He swung his sword rapidly, striking blow after blow at Meliadus, who parried as swiftly. Meliadus's face was twisted in an expression resembling that of the wolf helmet he had lost, and a hatred burned from his eyes that matched Hawkmoon's own.

Their swords clanged rhythmically in warlike harmony, each blow blocked, each blow returned, and it seemed that they would continue in this way until one dropped from weariness. But then a group of fighting warriors backed against Hawkmoon's horse and caused it to rear, throwing him backward so that he lost his footing in his stirrups, and Meliadus grinned and thrust at Hawkmoon's undefended chest. The blow lacked force, but it was enough to push Hawkmoon from his saddle. He fell to the ground below the hoofs of Meliadus's horse.

He rolled away as the baron tried to trample him, dragged himself to his feet, and did his best to defend himself from the volley of blows rained down on him by the triumphant Granbretanian.

Twice Meliadus's sword struck the helmet of Agonosvos, denting it badly. Hawkmoon felt the Jewel begin to pulse afresh. He shouted wordlessly and dashed in close.

Astonished by this unexpected move, Meliadus was taken off-guard, and his attempt to block Hawkmoon's thrust was only half-successful. Hawkmoon's sword cut a great furrow along one side of Meliadus's unprotected head, and his whole face seemed to open up and gush blood, his mouth crooked with pain and paralysis. He tried to wipe the blood from his eyes, and Hawkmoon grasped his sword arm and hauled him down to the ground. Meliadus wrenched himself free, stumbled backward, then rushed at Hawkmoon, his sword a blur of metal, striking Hawkmoon's blade with such force that both swords snapped.

For a moment the panting antagonists stood still, glaring at

one another; then each drew a long dirk from his belt, and they began to circle, poised to strike. Meliadus's handsome features were handsome no longer, and if he lived, would always bear the mark of Hawkmoon's blow. Blood still came plentifully from the wound, trickling down his breastplate.

Hawkmoon, for his part, was wearying rapidly. The wound he had sustained the day before was beginning to trouble him, and his head was on fire with the pain the Jewel caused. He could hardly see for it, and twice he staggered, only to right himself as Meliadus feinted with his dagger.

Then both men moved and were instantly locked together, grappling desperately to stab the single mortal blow that would end their feud.

Meliadus struck at Hawkmoon's eye but misjudged his blow, and the dagger scraped down the side of the helmet. Hawkmoon's dagger sliced toward Meliadus's throat, but the baron's hand came up, caught Hawkmoon's wrist, and turned it.

The dance of death went on as they wrestled, chest to chest, to deal the finishing cut. Their breath groaned from their throats, their bodies ached with weariness, but fierce hatred glared from both pairs of eyes still and would glare on until one or both became glazed in death.

Around them the battle continued, with Queen Frawbra's forces driving the enemy farther and farther back. Now none fought near the two men and only corpses surrounded them.

Dawn was beginning to touch the sky.

Meliadus's arm trembled as Hawkmoon tried to force it back and make the hand release his wrist. His own free hand was weakening on Meliadus's forearm, for this was his wounded side.

Despairingly, Hawkmoon brought his armoured knee up into Meliadus's armoured groin and shoved. The baron staggered. His foot caught in the harness of one of the slain, and he fell. Trying to struggle up, he became worse entangled, and his eyes filled with fear as Hawkmoon slowly advanced, himself only barely able to remain upright.

Hawkmoon raised his dagger. Now his head was swimming. He flung himself down at the baron, then felt a great weakness seize him, and the dagger dropped from his hand.

Blindly, he groped for the weapon, but consciousness was going. He gasped with anger, but even that emotion was ebbing. Fatalistically he knew that Meliadus would now be able to kill him at his very moment of triumph.

6

SERVANT OF THE RUNESTAFF

Hawkmoon peered through the eyeslits of the helmet, blinking in the bright light. His head still burned, but the anger and desperation seemed to have left him. He turned his neck and saw Oladahn and the Warrior in Jet and Gold staring down at him. Oladahn's face was concerned, but the warrior's face was still hidden by that enigmatic helm.

"I am not . . . dead?" Hawkmoon said weakly.

"It does not seem so," replied the warrior laconically. "Though perhaps you are."

"Merely exhausted," Oladahn said hastily, darting a disapproving glance at the mysterious warrior. "The wound in your arm has been dressed and is likely to heal quickly."

"Where am I?" Hawkmoon asked now. "A room . . ."

"A room in Queen Frawbra's palace. The city is hers again and the enemy slain, captured, or fled. We found your body sprawled across that of Baron Meliadus. We thought you both dead at first."

"So Meliadus is dead!"

"It is likely. When we returned to look for his corpse it had vanished. Doubtless it was borne away by some of his fleeing men."

"Ah, dead at last," said Hawkmoon thankfully. Now that Meliadus had paid for his crimes, he felt suddenly at peace, in spite of the pain that still pulsed in his brain. Another thought came to him. "Malagigi. You must find him. Tell him . . ."

"Malagigi is on his way. When he heard of your exploits he decided to call at the palace."

"Will he help me?"

"I do not know," Oladahn said, glancing again at the Warrior in Jet and Gold.

A little later Queen Frawbra entered, and behind her was the wizen-faced sorcerer carrying an object covered by a cloth. It was about the size and shape of a man's head.

"Lord Malagigi," Hawkmoon murmured, trying to rise from his bed.

"You are the young man who has been pursuing me in recent days? I cannot see your face in that helmet." Malagigi spoke waspishly, and Hawkmoon began to despair again.

"I am Dorian Hawkmoon. I proved my friendship to Hamadan. Meliadus and Nahak are destroyed, their forces gone."

"Hmm?" Malagigi frowned. "I have been told of this jewel thing in your head. I know about such creations and their properties. But whether it is *possible* to remove its power I cannot say . . ."

"I was told you were the only man who could do it," Hawkmoon said.

"Could—yes. Can? I do not know. I am growing old. Physically, I am not sure if . . ."

The Warrior in Jet and Gold stepped forward and touched Malagigi upon the shoulder. "You know me, sorcerer?"

Malagigi nodded. "Aye, I do."

"And you know the Power I serve?"

"Aye." Malagigi frowned, glancing from one to the other. "But what has that to do with this young man?"

"He, too, serves that Power, though he knows it not."

Malagigi's expression became instantly resolute. "Then I will help him," he said firmly, "even if it means risking my own life."

Again Hawkmoon raised himself on the bed. "What does all this mean? Whom do I serve? I was unaware . . ."

Malagigi withdrew the cloth from the object he carried. It was a globe covered with little irregularities, each of which glowed a different colour. The colours shifted constantly, making Hawkmoon blink rapidly.

"First you must concentrate," Malagigi told him, holding the strange globe close to his head. "Stare into the device. Stare hard. Stare long. Stare, Dorian Hawkmoon, at all the colours . . ."

Hawkmoon now found that he was no longer blinking, found that he could not tear his gaze away from the rapidly changing colours in the globe. A peculiar feeling of weightlessness overcame him. A great sensation of well-being. He began to smile, and then all became misty and it seemed he hung in a soft, warm mist, beyond space, beyond time. He was still absolutely conscious in one way, and yet he was unaware of the world around him.

For a long time he remained in this state, knowing vaguely that his body, which no longer seemed very much a part of him, was being moved from one place to another.

The delicate colours of the mist changed sometimes, from a shade of rose-red to shades of sky-blue and buttercup-yellow, but that was all he saw, and he felt nothing at all. He felt at peace, as he had never felt before, save perhaps as a small child in his mother's arms.

Then the pastel shades began to be shot through with veins of darker, grimmer colours, and the sense of peace was gradually lost as lightnings of black and blood-red zigzagged across his eyes. He felt a wrenching sensation, one of terrible agony, and he screamed aloud.

Then he opened his eyes to stare in horror at the machine before him. It was identical to the one he had seen so long ago in the palace laboratories of King Huon.

Was he back in Londra?

The webs of black, gold, and silver murmured to him, but they did not caress him as they had done before; instead, they contracted, moving away from him, growing tighter and tighter together until they filled only a fraction of the space. Hawkmoon stared around him and saw Malagigi and beyond him the laboratory where, earlier, he had rescued the sorcerer from the Dark Empire's men.

Malagigi looked exhausted, but there was an expression of great self-satisfaction on his old face.

He stepped forward with a metal box, gathered up the machine of the Black Jewel, and tossed it into the box, closing the lid firmly and locking it.

"The machine," Hawkmoon said thickly. "How did you get it?"

"I made it," Malagigi smiled. "Made it, Duke Hawkmoon, aye! It took a week of intensive effort while you lay there, partly protected from the other machine—the one in Londra—by my spells. I thought for a while that I had lost the struggle, but this morning the machine was complete, save for one element . . ."

"What was that?"

"Its life force. That was the crucial issue—whether I could time the spell aright. You see, I had to let the whole of the life of the Black Jewel come through and fill your mind, then hope that this machine would absorb it before it could begin to eat."

Hawkmoon smiled in relief. "And it did!"

"It did. You are now free from that fear, at any rate."

"Human dangers I can accept and meet cheerfully," Hawkmoon said, lifting himself from the couch. "I am in your debt, Lord Malagigi. If I can do you any service . . ."

"Nay—nothing," Malagigi said, almost with a smirk. "I am glad to have this machine here." He tapped the box. "Perhaps it will be of use to me sometime. Besides . . ." He frowned, staring thoughtfully at Hawkmoon.

"What is it?"

"Ah, nothing." Malagigi shrugged.

Hawkmoon touched his forehead. The Black Jewel was still embedded there, but it was cold. "You did not remove the Jewel?"

"No, though it could be done if you desire. It offers you no danger. It would be a simple matter of surgery to cut it from your head."

Hawkmoon was about to ask Malagigi how this could be arranged, when a thought came to him. "No," he said at length. "No, let it remain—a symbol of my hatred for the Dark Empire. I hope they will soon learn to fear that symbol."

"You intend to carry on the fight against them, then?"

"Aye—with redoubled effort now that you have freed me."

"It is a force that should be countered," Malagigi said. He drew a deep breath. "Now I must sleep. I am very tired. You will find your friends awaiting you in the courtyard."

Hawkmoon walked down the steps of the house into the bright, warm sunshine of the early day, and there was Oladahn, a smile splitting his furry face almost in two. Beside him was the tall figure of the Warrior in Jet and Gold.

"You are completely well?" asked the warrior.

"Completely."

"Good. Then I will leave you. Farewell, Dorian Hawkmoon."

"I thank you for your help," Hawkmoon said as the warrior began to stride toward his great white battle charger. Then, as the warrior began to mount, a memory returned and he said, "Wait."

"What is it?" The helmed head turned to regard him.

"It was you who convinced Malagigi he should remove the power of the Black Jewel. You told him that I serve the Power that you serve. Yet I know of no Power that is my master."

"You will know of it one day."

"What is the Power you serve?"

"I serve the Runestaff," said the Warrior in Jet and Gold, and he rattled the white horse's bridle, urging his mount through the gate and away before Hawkmoon could ask him further questions.

"The Runestaff, is it?" Oladahn murmured, frowning. "A myth, I thought . . ."

"Aye, a myth. I believe that warrior enjoys mysteries. Doubtless he jokes with us." Hawkmoon grinned, slapping Oladahn on the shoulder. "If we see him again, we'll get the truth from him. I'm hungry. A good dinner . . ."

"There's a banquet prepared at Queen Frawbra's palace." Oladahn winked. "The finest I've seen. And I think the queen's interest in you is not sparked merely by gratitude."

"Say you so? Well, I hope I do not disappoint her, friend Oladahn, for I am pledged to a fairer maid than Frawbra."

"Is it possible?"

"Aye. Come, little friend—let's enjoy the queen's food and make preparations to return to the West."

"Must we leave so soon? We're heroes here, and besides, we deserve a rest, surely?"

Hawkmoon smiled. "Stay yourself, if you will. But I've a wedding to attend—my own."

"Oh, well," sighed Oladahn in mock grief, "I could not miss that event. I suppose I will have to cut short my stay in Hamadan."

Queen Frawbra herself escorted them to the gates of Hamadan the next morning. "You'll not think again, Dorian Hawkmoon? I offer you a throne—the throne my brother died trying to win."

Hawkmoon looked to the west. Two thousand miles and several months' journey away, Yisselda awaited him, not knowing whether he had succeeded in his goal or was now a victim of the Black Jewel. Count Brass, too, waited and must be told of Granbretan's further infamy. Bowgentle, doubtless, was even now standing with Yisselda in the turret of the topmost tower of Castle Brass, looking over the wild fenland of Kamarg, trying to console the girl who wondered if the man pledged to wed her would ever return.

He bowed in his saddle and kissed the queen's hand. "I thank you, Your Majesty, and I am honoured that you should think me worthy to rule with you, but there is a pledge I must keep—that I would forfeit twenty thrones to keep—and I must go. Also my blade is needed against the Dark Empire."

"Then go," she said sadly, "but remember Hamadan and her queen."

"I will."

He urged his great blue-coated stallion out across the rocky plain. Behind him, Oladahn turned, blew a kiss to Queen Frawbra, winked, and rode after his friend.

Dorian Hawkmoon, Duke von Köln, rode steadily westward to claim his love and take his vengeance.